JESSIE'S WORDS WERE DROWNED OUT BY GUNFIRE...

erupting from the rustlers' campsite. One of the rustlers made a zigzag run for the campfire, firing his pistol as he did so. Jessie levered a round into her Winchester and sighted down on the runner. She squeezed the trigger just as the man reached the campfire. As the rifle butt thudded against her shoulder, she saw the rustler clutch at his neck and spin to the ground...

Also in the **LONE STAR** series
from Jove

LONGARM AND THE LONE STAR LEGEND
LONE STAR ON THE TREACHERY TRAIL
LONE STAR AND THE OPIUM RUSTLERS
LONE STAR AND THE BORDER BANDITS
LONE STAR AND THE KANSAS WOLVES
LONE STAR AND THE UTAH KID

A JOVE BOOK

LONE STAR AND THE LAND GRABBERS

A Jove Book/published by arrangement with
the author

PRINTING HISTORY
Jove edition/December 1982

ISBN: 0-515-06231-6

Jove books are published by Jove Publications, Inc.,
200 Madison Avenue, New York, N. Y. 10016. The words
"A JOVE BOOK" and the "J" with sunburst are trademarks
belonging to Jove Publications, Inc.

PRINTED IN THE UNITED STATES OF AMERICA

LONE STAR
AND THE LAND GRABBERS

★

Chapter 1

Ki leaned against the jamb of the general store's open doorway and watched the sun go down. He was in a town called Skinny Creek. It was just one short street, lined with a few buildings. Skinny Creek was a cowtown, like the dozen or so others scattered beneath the big Wyoming sky in 1880.

Skinny Creek was not on any map. Its places of business and its private residences were as scarce as the teeth in an old prospector's mouth. All the town had was the general store Ki was now standing in, a blacksmith's stable, a barber who also claimed to have some skill at pulling bad teeth, and a one-room flophouse for those cowboys passing through who had grown tired of sleeping under the stars, and wanted a roof over their heads.

Skinny Creek was even lacking a real saloon, as Ki had been sorry to discover. If a cowboy wanted a drink, he could buy one at the general store.

Long ago, the cowtown's buildings had been brightly painted, but the candy colors had been long since worn away by the sand-laden winds howling off the plains, as well as blistered off by the sun. Good cattle country was a day's ride to the northwest, toward the foothills of the Rockies. There the grass was green and lush, and the streams bubbled crystal-clear and sweet. Cowboys riding toward the mountains often had needs to be met before making that final push to their destination. Be it a shave and a haircut, tinned food, fresh cartridges, or a fresh bottle of whiskey, Skinny Creek met those needs.

The sky began to take on a pink and gray stain as the sun sank behind the mesas to the west. Those sheared-off hills looked close by, but they were more than three hours' ride away. Somewhere in the midst of them was the campsite where Ki was to meet Jessica Starbuck tomorrow morning.

The purple shadows lengthened and deepened. It was that twilight time before the sun had completely set and the stars could emerge. There was nothing more to see.

"Care for a drink to celebrate the evening?"

Ki turned to regard the proprietor, who had just spoken. "Shouldn't we wait for your husband to join us?" he asked quietly.

"My husband!" the woman chuckled, polishing the worn but clean countertop with a rag. "Don't reckon he'll be around, unless this be Halloween. He passed from this world over five years ago."

"But you still wear your wedding band," Ki pointed out.

"That I do, cowboy," the woman grinned, her pale blue eyes sparkling. "I've found that the gleam of a gold ring 'round a woman's finger takes the starch out of a man right quick. Since my man died—the scarlet fever took him, Lord rest his soul, 'cause I never gave him rest while he was with me—anyway, since he died, I put in this here bar." She gestured over her shoulder to the wooden shelf lined with whiskey bottles. "Now there isn't a thing a cowboy can't buy here, 'cept the remedy for that certain itch a male gets after a few days rubbing against a saddle." She brushed back her shoulder-length, raven-black hair, and sighed wistfully as she looked Ki up and down. "There are some things a lady doesn't sell . . ."

Ki blushed, "I'm surprised a lady as pretty as you hasn't found another husband."

"Oh, you!" the woman giggled. "Aren't you the one to talk, though. You make a pretty picture, yourself. My name's Mary Hudson, by the by," she added, winking at Ki. She turned to select a whiskey bottle from her shelf, and set it down on the counter, along with two glasses. "You just earned yourself a free drink, cowboy."

"Thanks," Ki said, removing his gray Stetson as he approached the counter. "My name is Ki—"

"Thought so!" Mary cried. "You're somewhat Chinese, aren't you?"

Ki sighed wearily. "My mother was Japanese, but my father was an American—

"Japanese, eh?" Mary cocked her head to one side, and then grinned. "What's that they say? That mixed breeds make the smartest ponies and hounds?" She wiggled free the cork in the bottle, and then poured them both a generous measure of sour mash. "Well, don't you worry, Ki," she comforted. "Reckon if it's true for horses and dogs, it's true for folks as well. I'll say this for you, you sure came out handsome, whatever the mix."

Ki turned away to hide his amusement. This woman was in her thirties, but she had the brash, childlike manner of a girl half her age. Ki was a samurai, a professional warrior who had been trained in the martial arts before he had left his homeland. Any *man* who had dared to equate Ki with dogs and horses would have encountered a samurai's wrath, but Mary's ingenuous chatter, impertinent as it was, seemed inoffensive, even friendly.

"After all," Mary ran on, handing Ki his drink, "you're tall, aren't you?"

Ki nodded.

"Hmmmm," Mary said dreamily. "And you've got such wide shoulders and a flat belly. And that long black hair of yours, and those brown, slanted eyes—why, your eyes are the only part of you that even looks Chi—uh, *Japanese*." Raising her glass, she swallowed down her whiskey in one nervous gulp. "Don't know what's gotten into me," she muttered, half to herself. "Never took such liberties with a man before." She shrugged. "But I never met a part-Japanese fellow before."

"Excellent bourbon," Ki said. He put a half-dollar on the counter. "I'll buy the next drink." He perused the bottles lining the shelf. "Would you have some Scotch?"

"Everything but," Mary apologized. "Got to go to Nettle Grove for Scotch whiskey."

Ki nodded. Nettle Grove was a much larger, bona fide township, located in cattle country, a day's ride to the west. "Sour mash will do, then. You *do* seem to sell everything else."

He looked around. Most every foot of wall and floor space was taken up with displays of the store's goods and wares. One case held nothing but canned vittles—ham, sardines, tomatoes, and the like. There were open sacks of coffee, sugar, salt, and flour propped against each other beneath the shelves of brightly labeled tinned goods. The half-filled sacks drooped like drunks holding each other up beneath a lamppost. There were bins of nails, soap, crackers, and dried beans. Coils of new rope, stiff as wire, and clusters of canteens hung from long wooden wall pegs. Shelves of new denim pants and folded flannel shirts kept the ropes and canteens company. Behind the counter, next to the whiskey, were two racks of firearms. A chain snaked through the levers of the shiny new, expensive Winchester .44-40s, as well as through the lower-priced, used Henry repeaters. Chains were also laced through the trigger guards of the various Colt and Smith & Wesson pistols, to protect them against pilferage. Beneath the guns, piled upon a stack of blankets, were boxes of ammunition.

A full-length mirror propped against the wall, right below the shelves of new clothing, caught Ki's eye, with his own reflection.

The samurai was dressed in his usual "working outfit": tight-fitting, worn denims; a collarless pullover shirt of cotton twill; and a well-broken-in, sleeveless brown leather vest lined with many inside pockets. Ki usually preferred to go hatless and barefoot. The soles of his feet were leather-tough from the years he'd spent perfecting his *te,* or "empty hand" skills—the blocks, kicks, and strikes of unarmed combat. This time, however, Ki wanted to blend in with his surroundings as much as possible. Accordingly, he was wearing low-cut Wellington boots, a gunbelt, and his gray Stetson. The suit that matched the Stetson—his traveling and "city" suit—was hanging in the closet of his Nettle Grove hotel room. He and Jessie had arrived there by train a week ago. Then they'd rented horses and set out to do some exploration of the range country. The nearest Starbuck office, located in Colorado, had informed Jessie that some of the smaller ranches, new to the area, were having trouble with rustlers and competition from the bigger, already established spreads. When Jessie was told that the smaller ranchers were looking for partners who could bring them operating funds, she became interested in the business aspects of the situation. Especially since she'd been told that the Prussian cartel had joined forces with the largest cattle baron in the territory . . .

"Now that I look at you," Mary began, gazing at Ki, "I can see that you're no drover, after all."

Now it was Ki's turn to peruse the storekeeper. She was dressed in a long calico skirt and a light blue chambray work shirt. She was tall, and built lean, for the Wyoming Territory's way of life tended to burn the excess fat off both women and men. Yet she had full, round breasts and a saucy backside that kept her thin cloth skirt nicely filled out.

"You couldn't be a lawman," Mary persisted. "Are you a bounty hunter?" Her pale blue eyes were now open wide.

Ki sipped at his drink as he tried to think of a way to answer her question. He was here in Skinny Creek because this was where he'd tracked those rustlers. He was here because Jessie believed these cattle thieves were indirectly working for the cartel.

At times like this, he wondered if the bloody war between

Jessie and the ruthless Prussians who had murdered her parents would ever end. The cartel was everywhere; Jessie's father, Alex Starbuck, had first encountered it in the Orient, and its tentacles reached even into the remote frontier of America. The cartel was like a venomous, many-headed snake. Each time Jessie and Ki cut off one of those heads, another would appear. Were even the vast resources of the Starbuck business empire—commanded now by Jessie since the death of her father—enough to stop the evil?

It was the Denver offices of Starbuck Enterprises that had uncovered this latest viper's nest of the cartel. In attempting to establish a cattlemen's cooperative among the smaller ranchers of this area in Wyoming Territory, they'd found that the ranchers were being plagued by large-scale rustling of their stock. Suspecting that the cattle thievery might have been instigated by larger cattle interests, the Denver offices had done some research that revealed that the owner of the largest spread hereabouts was a man named Tom Schiff. Further probing into Schiff's background turned up financial ties with the cartel's cattle interests.

None of this was conclusive, of course, but it had been enough to persuade Jessie to leave the Circle Star Ranch in Texas and undertake the difficult rail journey to Wyoming Territory. Ki, as her bodyguard and companion, had accompanied her.

The one thing that had confounded both Jessie and Ki was why, if the cartel already had a chunk of Schiff's huge spread, the Prussians felt it necessary to try and steal away the tiny spreads staked out by the new ranchers. A few days of prospecting around the newer ranchers' land had answered that question. Jessie and Ki had found indications of huge underground coal deposits. Someday the railroad was going to come deeper into Wyoming, and when it did, it was going to need that coal. The Prussians meant to have the coal for their own, even if they had to steal and murder for it.

Jessie Starbuck meant for that coal to remain in the hands of the small ranchers who had staked out the land. They were the legal owners of the mineral rights.

The plan had been for Ki to trail the rustlers while Jessie began negotiations with the leader of the small ranchers, a man named Hiram Tang. His spread was West of Skinny Creek, closer to the township of Nettle Grove. The mesas where Ki was to meet Jessie tomorrow morning were half-way to Tang's ranch.

Right now, as Ki evaded Mary's questions with silent shrugs, he was hoping that Jessie had met with better luck than had come to him. The rustlers' tracks seemed to disappear right here in Skinny Creek. Where in these few ramshackle buildings could a band of ten men—*and* their horses—be hiding?

"So you aren't talking, eh?" Mary chuckled, lighting a kerosene lantern against the darkness. "Well, that's all right. Lots of men in these parts like to keep their business to themselves."

Ki wanted to ask her if she knew anything of the whereabouts of the rustlers, but he hesitated. A samurai is trained to believe that the concept of honor is what is most important in life. Mary had asked him about his doings, and he had refused to tell her, thinking that only Jessie herself had the right to reveal that information. A samurai could not exclude a person from his confidence, and then ask for that person's help. That was not honorable.

"That your horse out there, Ki?" Mary asked.

Ki turned to look out through the open doorway, to where his chestnut gelding was being examined by two men. The horse was rented, but the saddle was Ki's own. It stored some of the weapons Ki used.

In Japan, a warrior was considered useless without a horse. Indeed, Ki now mused as he fitfully watched the two strangers fingering his belongings, the expression *kyūba no michi,* meaning "way of the bow and horse," aptly summed up the samurai's way of living his life. *Bajutsu,* the technique of horsemanship, was considered a *kakuto bugei*, or fighting technique equal in importance to the thirty-odd other *bugei* Ki had studied and mastered.

Just then the larger of the two began to unstrap the flap of one of Ki's saddle bags. The samurai felt anger pulse through him. For another to presume to open his property without permission was intolerable.

"Hold on now," Mary warned in a low whisper, as if she had read Ki's thoughts. "Those two don't mean nothing, and anyway, the big one there, fella by the name of Len Vickers, is only here to see me. Got some fool idea about sparking me . . ."

"Do you care for him?" Ki asked, his dark brown, almond-shaped eyes still on the two men.

"For Len?" Mary snorted. "The way I care for a dog with hydrophobia. The thing is, you've got to handle Len just as carefully as a mad animal. I've been putting him off, but I've got to do it gently, else he might just take what he wants from me without asking."

Ki turned in time to catch Mary's shudder of disgust and fear. "I'm glad that you do not care for him," Ki began. "I think this night will see the mad dog put down."

"Now don't you go looking for trouble!" Mary hissed anxiously. "Len and his pal there, Dolan, work as regulators for some of those big spreads west of here."

"Regulators," Ki slowly repeated. "Then it is their job to see that no one steals their employer's cattle?"

"That, and to see that nobody else's cattle grazes on land claimed by their bosses," Mary explained. "Both of those men are fast with their pistols, and they ain't shy about using them," she warned, but then cut herself short as the two regulators entered the store.

"What the hell are *you,* boy?" the bigger man, Len, addressed Ki as he clomped his way across the floor's wooden planking. "There in your saddle boot, where a rifle ought to be, you've got a bow and arrows." The regulator now addressed his remarks to Mary. "Me and Dolan here thought we'd caught us one of them Utes who'd jumped the Ouray Reservation, over east of here. There's a band of 'em about, and they're bad ones. Shot up a family for the fun of it."

"He's no Indian," Mary remarked quietly.

"I can see that, woman," Len said gruffly. "What we got here is a Chinaman."

The two men were dressed in the simple garb of High Plains cattlemen. They wore patched and tattered canvas pants, solid gray flannel shirts, and flat-topped, sweat-stained Stetsons. Their boots were caked with dust and mud, and they wore their gunbelts high. Dolan's gun was on his right hip, but Len's was worn cavalry-officer style. His holster sat just to the left of his belt buckle. His pistol's butt was angled to the right. Len was a crossdraw man.

"Hey, Chinaman," Len teased. "I don't see your pigtail."

Dolan smirked but said nothing. He had a long-nosed, weak-chinned face, with darting yellow eyes somewhere in between the color of sand and piss. The samurai understood how it was between Len and Dolan. The smaller man was the larger's pet. In Japan, many samurai kept monkeys for their amusement.

"Why do you carry a bow and not a rifle, Chinaman?" Len asked.

"Let's us all have a drink," Mary said with forced good cheer, setting two more glasses down beside the pair already there, and filling each with sour mash.

Dolan hurried over to the counter, while Len sauntered along behind his pet. Ki also approached the counter where the drinks waited. He had no desire to drink with these men, but he wished no trouble, for Mary's sake.

"Hold on there, boy," Len snapped. "Chinamen can't have no good bourbon. They drink tea!"

Dolan laughed uproariously. He was standing between Len and Ki. "Tea!" he gasped. "Yessir, tea!" He reached out to snatch away Ki's glass, and drank it down himself.

Ki let him. It looked like there was going to be a fight after all, the samurai realized. If so, it was to his advantage for Dolan to drink himself into slow reflexes and bad aim.

"Len, please," Mary begged now. "No trouble, please."

"Don't you worry, little lady," Len smirked. "You got tea, don't you, Mary? Fetch it."

The woman did nothing, but merely stared at Ki.

"Fetch it *now,* Mary," Len growled.

She shrugged helplessly and walked the length of the counter, coming back with a paper sack of tea leaves that she placed on the counter, beside the bottle of sour mash.

"I reckon we ain't got time to fix a cup o' tea, Chinaman," Len glowered at Ki. "You been messing with my woman? I'm gonna teach you a lesson. You just *eat* them leaves."

"He didn't do nothing, Len!" Mary begged.

"Shut up!" the regulator snapped. "Eat them leaves, boy," he again ordered Ki.

The samurai examined the man's face, trying to ascertain whether Len was bluffing. The regulator had small green eyes and scarred cheeks, long ago pitted by the pox, Ki guessed. Len's features had been baked red by the sun, and his nose pressed flat against his face, the result of some well-aimed blow with either fist or rifle butt. In all, he looked like a tough man, a man used to having his own way.

"I'm waiting," Len said softly. "Do it!"

Dolan moved out of the way. He walked to a big cracker barrel that stood in the middle of the floor, and helped himself to a few. Munching on the crackers, he moved to stand behind the waist-high barrel.

Len now stepped closer to Ki, so that less than two feet separated them. "I'm waiting," he repeated. His hand pushed the bag of tea in Ki's direction.

Ki shifted his stance to confront the regulator. The man was a few inches shorter than the samurai, but much more massively built. His chest and arm muscles tightly filled his gray flannel shirt. "You wait for nothing but your own death," Ki softly told Len. "You wait to die by pursuing this game with me." Out of the corner of his eye, Ki saw Dolan stiffen and begin to inch his hand toward his holster.

"I'm gonna nail your hide to the side of this here store," Len boasted. His right hand hovered over the butt of his pistol.

First disable Len to buy time, and then kill Dolan, Ki

calculated, while a sinking sensation in the pit of his belly warned him that the two regulators had positioned themselves cunningly. If the two men were indeed as fast with their guns as Mary had claimed, he himself was likely to take a wound . . .

Just then, Mary reached beneath the counter to come up with a shotgun. It was a double-barreled twelve-gauge, sawed off to a length of eighteen inches. The metallic rolling click of the two hammers being thumbed back filled the now silent store as she aimed the shotgun at Dolan.

"If this is gonna happen, it's gonna happen *fair!*" she decreed. "Stay out of it, Dolan."

"Hey," Dolan chuckled. He stared at Mary, and at the black snout of the shotgun pointed his way. "Hey," he repeated, as beads of sweat began to pop out upon his brow. He glanced quizzically at Len.

"Mary, you put that gun right back where you got it," Len growled.

"I swear I'll kill him, Len," she answered quickly, her voice tight with tension.

"I'll fix you for this, later!" Len swore at her. "Right after I—"

But he never finished his statement, instead choosing that moment to go for his gun. Ki's rigidly extended fingers struck out to execute a *yonhon-nukite-uchi,* or spear-hand strike. The tips of the samurai's steel-stiff fingers stabbed into Len's protruding gut, just above his belt buckle. Ki had channeled much focused energy into the jab. It felt to him as if the tips of his fingers had brushed against the regulator's backbone.

Len hissed out air like a punctured balloon. He began to double over. His pistol—a double-action .41-caliber Smith & Wesson—had been halfway drawn out of its angled holster. It now slid the rest of the way out of its sheath of waxed leather, to clatter to the floor.

The regulator's big hands were reaching out for Ki's throat. The samurai relaxed his fingers from their spear-hand tautness, and brought his hand up in a move the old teachers had dubbed the "fishtail", because the hand rose palm down, while the fingers trailed limply beneath. The movement suggested the stately grace of Japan's prized, fantailed goldfish.

As Ki's hand reached the level of Len's chin, the samurai snapped his wrist up, to whip his now rigid fingers across Len's mouth, and nose. Blood arced crimson from Len's face. A red froth of it misted from his already flat nose. The regulator toppled sideways to slam to the floor.

Was it instinct that caused Ki to turn toward Dolan, or had the samurai actually seen the man go for his gun? In any event, Ki was already reaching inside his vest to extract a *shuriken* throwing blade as Dolan began to bring up his battered-looking Colt Thunderer.

"No!" Mary screamed at Dolan. "I'll shoot!"

Now it was Dolan who was caught in a potential crossfire. He swiveled his yellow eyes from Ki to Mary, his gun wavering indecisively between the two.

Len jackknifed into a sitting position from his place on the floor, and pulled a derringer from the top of his boot.

Ki sent his *shuriken* throwing blade—a four-inch-long, razor-sharp knife without hilt or handle—streaking toward Len's heart. The *shuriken* found its target. The derringer spat its shot into the planking of the floor. Len cried out in agony as a red, wet flower blossomed upon his gray flannel shirt front. He stared down at the steel embedded in his chest, and then slumped backward, his last breath wheezing out of him as his body settled into death.

Dolan issued a panicked whine as he snapped off a shot in Ki's direction. The samurai felt the round's hot wind whistling past his ear. He was reaching for another *shuriken* blade when Mary closed her eyes and pulled both triggers of her shotgun.

There was a deep, deafening, double *boom!* The weapon's recoil jolted its wooden stock out of the woman's grasp. One load struck the cracker barrel, sending splinters of wood and a cloud of shattered crackers up as high as the ceiling. The other barrel caught Dolan square in the belly. His Colt flew away as if jerked from his grasp by a string. Dolan himself flew backward to hit the wall and then bounce forward, belly-flopping upon the shattered cracker barrel. Blood began to seep out from under what was now just a ruined corpse.

Except for the ticking of the wall clock, and Ki's and Mary's harsh breathing, the store was as silent as the tomb it had become for Len and Dolan. From outside came excited shouts and the thudding of boots. Those who had heard the shots were racing to see what had happened.

Mary, gazing down at Dolan's shotgun-ripped body sagging across the splintered barrel, murmured, "Crackers and jam . . ." Then she giggled in a manner that Ki thought was more than a trifle hysterical. Mary's eyelids fluttered. She had time to utter, "I'm feeling dizzy . . ." before slumping to the floor in a dead faint.

Ki had already pulled his *shuriken* blade from Len's chest. He wiped the steel clean on a patch of the dead man's shirt, and then slipped the throwing weapon back into its sheath, sewn into the lining of his vest. He crossed the store, leaped nimbly over the counter, and was picking Mary up, easily supporting her dead weight across his arms, as the first of the onlookers began to rubberneck through the store's open doorway.

"There's been trouble," Ki addressed the men who were now staring at him. "These two drew on us, and Mary and I were forced to kill them in self-defense." The samurai waited for somebody to say something, but they all just continued to stare silently at him. Mary began to stir in his arms. Ki suddenly became aware of her body, soft and warm against his chest.

"To whom shall I speak concerning this?" Ki demanded.

"Blacksmith moonlights as the undertaker," piped a helpful adolescent voice from the rear of the crowd.

"Here I am," called out a large man in a leather apron. He shouldered his way through the onlookers blocking the doorway, and began to examine the two bodies, going so far as to begin to measure their length with a cloth tape measure he pulled from his pocket. "Plain wood boxes?" he asked Ki.

The samurai ignored him. "I meant, is there any law here?"

Several men shrugged their shoulders. One said, "We got no town marshal. Nettle Grove has one, but I don't reckon he does much enforcing out of sight of that township's church steeple. There's a sheriff in the county seat of Cough Creek, but that'd be over a hundred and fifty miles due east of here. Ain't never seen that sheriff, but I hear tell there is one. Then we got a federal marshal in Denver, but I reckon he ain't gonna close up shop in Colorado for a week or so to make the trek to Skinny Creek—"

"Enough," Ki muttered. "What do you people do when a killing takes place?"

"Blacksmith moonlights as the undertaker," repeated that same young voice from the rear of the crowd.

The blacksmith grinned up at Ki. "That's my boy," he said.

Ki shifted Mary's weight to one arm and then dug into the pocket of his denims. He tossed several dollars to the floor, just in front of the blacksmith. "Then see to these two," he ordered.

"Their horses, guns, personal belongings?" the blacksmith asked. "They belong to you now, I reckon."

"I do not want them. Hold them for Mary."

"I'll do that for Mrs. Hudson," the blacksmith smiled. "Sure I will."

"Will your son earn himself a dollar by cleaning up this mess, and scrubbing clean the floor?" Ki asked.

"He will," the blacksmith replied. "And he'll see to your horse in the bargain."

Ki added another dollar to the pile of money on the floor, and then turned to carry Mary through the curtained doorway behind the counter. The samurai found himself in a rather spartan but clean sitting room. A threadbare sofa and three straight-backed chairs were grouped around a scarred, wooden table. Three candles, flickering in a tarnished silver candelabrum on the table, lit the room. Rose patterned wallpaper and braided throw rugs added to the sparse comforts. The wallpaper was now grimy and fly-specked, and the throw rugs were faded and in some spots worn through, but both decorations, along with the silver candelabrum testified to the past affluence of the Hudsons. Such luxuries had to be shipped, at great expense, from San Francisco or the East.

Ki continued through the railroad flat. He passed a small galley kitchen on his way to the last room. It was dark in here, but by the faint light cast by a sliver of moon glimmering through the single window, Ki could make out the shape of the widow's big double bed. Gently he set her down upon the coverlet and struck a match and, by its light, found another candle holder sitting on the woman's bureau. He lit the candles, and then glanced back at Mary to find her smiling up at him.

"I was sort of fooling you," she said shyly. "I came awake a few minutes ago."

"I know," Ki smiled. "I felt the change as you became conscious."

Blushing, Mary stuttered, "I—I didn't want to let go of you. Leave your arms, I mean..."

"Hush," Ki scolded her gently. He sat down next to her on the bed and gently caressed her cheek. "I did not want you to leave my arms."

Mary nodded happily. "It's been a long time since a man has been in this bed with me."

"It is not a concern," Ki promised. Freeing his hand, he began to unbutton her work shirt.

"But I want you to know," she persisted. "I don't want you to think I'm cheap. Despite what Len was hinting at, there's been no one in my bed since my husband—"

Ki did not answer, but bent his head to lick and suck at her firm, round breasts. Mary's nipples rose in response as he gently chewed them. The wet trail his tongue left across her fragrant cleavage glistened in the candles' glow.

"Ohhhh, God," she moaned. "It's been so long...sooo

long!" She began to squirm, tearing off her skirt as Ki tugged off her boots. Next came her white ruffled pantalets. Her fingers plucked frantically at the pink satin ribbons cinching them tight, and once they were loosened she wiggled the lacy undergarment down past her hips and shapely, bouncing bottom, like a snake shedding its skin.

Ki paused to gaze at her. "You are a very beautiful woman," he murmured, taking in her lean, trim figure. The dark triangle between her legs began to bead with moisture.

"You've got me so hot, just by looking at me with those dark eyes of yours!" Mary exclaimed excitedly. "Undress and get over here, or I swear I'll just die!"

Ki did as he was told while Mary pulled the coverlet off the bed. He waited until she had her back to him, and then quickly slid a *shuriken* blade from his vest, palming it as he approached the bed. As he climbed in beside her, he managed to slip the weapon beneath a pillow without her noticing his action. A naked man in a woman's embrace made an easy target, Ki knew. He wanted to be prepared in the unlikely event that Len and Dolan had some friends who might wish to even the score.

Mary leaped upon him hungrily. She straddled him, her fingers guiding his hardness into her wet, warm, center as her mouth locked against his. It seemed only seconds before she began to writhe and buck upon him, moaning, "I'm coming, I'm coming, I'm coming!" in a rising cadence that culminated in a catlike wail of gratification.

She began to use her internal muscles to squeeze and pull at Ki, and it wasn't long before he felt his own orgasm swelling him ever larger and larger, until it burst forth in a bubble of exquisitely paralyzing pleasure that turned his arms and legs to jelly. When he could, he wrapped his arms around her finely sculpted back, pressing himself to her.

"That was mighty fine, wasn't it now?" Mary asked tenderly, running her fingers through Ki's hair.

Ki sighed that it was. His fingers tickled the cleft of her jutting buttocks as he planted kisses along the satiny curve of her delicate jaw.

Mary giggled, her laugh silvery. She pressed her damp breasts against his chest and continued to knead his manhood with her internal muscles, sending shivery pulses of pleasure up and down his spine.

Soon Ki felt himself growing hard once again. He began to gyrate his hips beneath Mary, but she pulled free of him.

"Let's do it different this time," she begged. "Let's do it like horses do!" She got onto her hands and knees, pressing her face against the pillows and thrusting her tail high into the air.

Ki settled onto his knees behind her. He clasped her hips in his strong hands and entered her from the rear.

Mary squealed with pleasure as Ki thrust in and out, his ridged belly muscles rippling as his strokes increased in speed. Ki spread apart her bottom's cheeks. He wet his finger with saliva and gently pressed its tip into her anal opening. Mary arched her back and let loose an unintelligible series of mewls and moans. Her fingers dug furrows into her pillows as her splayed pink buttocks wiggled and contracted as if they were being spanked. When she came, she howled so loudly that Ki half-expected the blacksmith and his son to come running in here, thinking that yet another killing had taken place this night. Then Mary reached around to tickle his scrotum, and Ki stopped thinking. Now it was his turn to arch his back as he shot into her, pumping and pumping until he was certain that he had not another drop left to give her.

They fell asleep in each other's arms. Ki dozed soundly until the first faint gray glow of dawn poked its way through the bedroom's window. He gingerly untangled himself from her embrace, and got out of bed in order to dress. Mary stirred, and came awake.

"You're leaving . . ." she mumbled, her voice thick with sleep. She sat up, her naked breasts rising free from the tops of the blankets. "Of course you're leaving," she said sadly.

Ki noticed a framed tintype on her bureau. By the dawn light he saw a sandy-haired man with pleasant, regular features, and a towheaded boy of no more than ten smiling out at him. *A son,* Ki thought. "You did not mention that you have a son," he said as he finished dressing.

Mary shrugged. "The fever took him the same time it took his daddy," she replied. Then she gave Ki a sad but proud ghost of a smile. "Folks tend to pity widows enough as it is, no call for me to go wearing my heart on my sleeve in carrying on about my Stevie. He was a good boy, though."

Ki knelt by the bed. He took her hand and gently squeezed it. "You are a strong woman," he said sincerely. "I compliment you on your sense of honor."

"You do talk right funny," Mary said gruffly, but her pale blue eyes suddenly grew shiny. "No call to make a fuss. Things change, is all. They come and they go. Take this town, for instance. Skinny Creek wasn't always just a stopping place for cowhands passing through," she explained. "When my husband and son and I came here, it was an up-and-coming mining town. Yessir, there was a big silver mine." She shrugged. "'Course, the vein petered out. That's when the scarlet fever hit. That pretty much finished Skinny Creek's hopes for a bright future."

And yours as well, Ki added silently. "Why do you stay here?" he asked.

"Why not?" Mary countered wryly. "Oh, sure, I could go to a larger town, but my whole life—my menfolk—are buried here. Sometimes, when I ride or stroll out beyond the town, I think I can see them both riding toward me." She smiled at the samurai. "I guess you think that's silly," she mumbled.

"In my homeland, those spirits are called *kami,*" Ki replied. "In Japan it is thought that the spirits of our dead ancestors and relatives watch over us." He rose from his place by the side of the bed, and bent to kiss her forehead. "I do not think that what you have said is silly."

Mary nodded. "I'll fix you some breakfast?" she offered.

"Stay in bed," Ki urged. "I am not hungry."

"I can't. I got to clean up that—that *mess* in the store." She shuddered.

"It's been done. I hired the blacksmith's son to do the task," Ki told her, also explaining that the blacksmith was holding the dead men's property for her.

"Most men rent, but I know for a fact that Len and Dolan owned their own horses," she smiled. "Those mounts and their saddles will fetch me a right nice piece of money. I'm grateful to you, Ki."

Standing before her, Ki nodded. "Well, then, goodbye," he said.

"Goodbye," Mary said quietly. "Reckon you know that if your business ever brings you this way again—"

"I know," Ki smiled. "Go back to sleep, Mary." He turned and left the bedroom, passing through the sitting room and pausing in the store to make sure that the boy had indeed done his job. Except for a few damp scrub marks on the floor, there was nothing to indicate the deaths that had taken place last night.

He found the blacksmith's son dozing in the stable. The boy came awake as Ki finished saddling his horse.

"I would've done that for you, mister!" he exclaimed.

"I prefer doing it myself," Ki replied. "You did a good job in the store," he added.

The boy grinned. "Gee, mister, for a dollar, you could've asked me to paint the place!"

Ki led his chestnut gelding out of the stable, mounted up, and rode off. He was some miles out of Skinny Creek before he realized that he'd forgotten the *shuriken* blade he'd placed beneath Mary's pillow. Well, he had plenty of other throwing blades, and Jessie was waiting for him.

The samurai smiled to himself. Besides, now he had an excuse to pass this way again.

★

Chapter 2

Ki's mount loped along in an easy, steady gait that ate up the miles. As the flat-topped mesas grew ever larger in the crystal-clear, invigorating Wyoming air, the rust-red ground with its prickly grass gave way to granite outcroppings, patches of sparse but somewhat green grass, and stands of scrubby cottonwoods. This was not yet good grazing land, Ki knew, but it was the start of cattle country. On the other side of those hills, presided over by the mountains that stood like a dark purple wall in the distance, were lush green meadows and sparkling clear brooks of icy water.

A thin, curling skein of smoke began to rise up into the early morning air from somewhere in the center of the mesas. Ki frowned. It was not like Jessie to be so careless. If he could track her position by means of that smoke, so could the cattle rustlers whose trail he'd lost at Skinny Creek.

The samurai needn't have worried. Once he'd reached the campfire he found just that—a campfire, and nothing else. As he dismounted, Ki heard the metallic sound of a hammer being lowered. Up popped Jessie from behind a large boulder, her Colt in her hand.

Her brown Stetson was dangling on her back, held in place by its leather thong around her neck, to reveal a tawny mane of honey-blonde hair glinting with a hint of copper beneath the strong Wyoming sun. Each time Ki saw her he was struck anew by how lovely Jessie was.

She stood easy in her low-heeled, brown cordovan leather boots, resting one hand on her hip, clasping her Colt loosely in the other. "What took you so long?" she asked Ki, her voice merry with relief and her green eyes flashing welcome. "I was beginning to grow worried."

"I was unavoidably detained," Ki remarked, and then filled Jessie in on last night's events in Skinny Creek, leaving out the details of his evening of pleasure in Mary Hudson's bed. All the while Ki spoke, his almond eyes took in Jessie's form. She was in her twenties. Long-legged, she had high, full breasts, a slender waist accented by the gunbelt she wore, and a firm, plushly rounded bottom. None of her figure was the least bit hidden by her tight denim jeans, white silk blouse, and wrangler's waist-length denim jacket. The clothes fit her like a second skin.

As he spoke, the samurai felt the heat rising in his loins. Angrily he pushed his lewd thoughts concerning Jessie away. They were not honorable. Ki had come to the Starbuck ranch in Texas when he was just an adolescent. Jessie's father had hired the young samurai on as Jessie's bodyguard. As much as Ki loved Jessie, he knew he had to keep his passionate feelings buried deep within him. For Jessie to suspect that Ki had anything more than brotherly feelings of affection toward her would mean that he had failed in his samurai vows. Other men could and did enjoy Jessie's embrace, but never Ki himself, for to do so could mean that he might allow his guard to drop as her protector.

"How did you do in those two regulators?" Jessie now asked. She gestured with her Colt toward the gunbelt cinched around Ki's waist. "I know you didn't use that!" she laughed, her green eyes as bewitching as a cat's.

Ki smiled. "No. I used a *shuriken* on the one I killed. As I told you, the woman storekeeper shot the other." He unstrapped his holstered gun and stuffed the weapon into his saddlebag. "You know I never keep this old Peacemaker of mine loaded," he said.

"Oh, that's right," Jessie grinned. "I forgot that samurai warriors were afraid of guns." Of course she knew better than that; the Japanese had firearms early in the fifteenth century. But Jessie loved to tease Ki. She took the sassy but innocent pleasure in it that a younger sister takes in getting and keeping the attention of a much-loved, much-worshipped brother. Jessie could not imagine what her life would have been like without Ki. Much shorter, certainly! The samurai had saved her life countless times.

"We are not afraid of firearms, but merely disdainful of them," Ki argued, playing along. "They are such noisy, messy things. And so crude!"

"This Colt? Crude?" Jessie exclaimed. "How dare you? I'm thankful my daddy isn't alive to hear you say that!" she joshed. She slid her gun into its waxed holster, which she wore just to the rear of her shapely right hip.

Ki could not keep from laughing. "My apologies to your pistol," he managed to say.

"My Colt and I shall consider it," Jessie said, and then giggled. It was true that her pistol was a remarkable, one-of-a-kind weapon. Her father had taught Jessie how to shoot, but her slender, graceful, feminine hand had found her father's double-action Colt .44's recoil too much for her. During one of his business trips back East, Alex Starbuck had visited the Colt factory in Connecticut. There he'd commissioned a very special gift for his daughter's eighteenth birthday. The pistol's cylinder was chambered for .38 shells, but mounted on a double-action .44 frame. This reduced the handgun's recoil to the point where Jessie could squeeze off several rounds—very accurately—before her father could fire more than two from his own hefty .44. The Colt, finished in slate gray, with grips of polished peachwood, was more than just a weapon. It was a cherished memento from her late father. She had to admit, though, that when it came to getting herself out of tough scrapes, she usually relied more on the surprise generated by the sudden appearance of her ivory-gripped, double-barreled .38-caliber derringer. When she was wearing a skirt, Jessie usually kept the little gun in a garter-belt holster, high on her thigh. When she was wearing denims, she kept the backup gun nestled behind her belt buckle, or tucked into the top of her boot.

"You know, Ki," Jessie now taunted, "You really shouldn't dismiss the effectiveness of firearms. Why, by your own account, you would have been in a very tight spot if this woman friend of yours hadn't produced that shotgun."

"My point precisely," Ki began to lecture. "To skillfully use a samurai's weapons takes years of practice, great concentration, and, most important, a noble warrior's spirit." With that said, Ki turned away.

Jessie waited a moment in silence. "So?" she finally demanded, hating herself for asking, but unable to resist taking the bait. "So?"

"So," Ki replied, his back still to her, and his tone slightly bored. "So last night proves that *anybody* can use a gun!"

"My apologies to your noble warrior's spirit," Jessie intoned. Then, chuckling, she said, "It's good to see you."

"And you," Ki answered, turning to face her. Now his voice was carefully controlled, and his eyes seemed watchful. "As I have said," he began, changing the subject, "I tracked the rustlers for some days before losing them at Skinny Creek. I feel that they were, or are, still there."

"And yet you couldn't find them or their hideout," Jessie frowned thoughtfully.

"I searched every building," the samurai explained. "I could not find the men. Their horses were not in the town's only stable."

"Well," Jessie said, "I had better luck. I spent my time at Hiram Tang's spread. His attorney in Nettle Grove produced papers certifying that Mr. Tang has the authority to negotiate for the other small ranchers."

"Do we need the others?" Ki asked.

"It's true that Tang's acreage is greater than the others," Jessie agreed. "And he's got most of the coal deposits, but if we include all of the small ranches in the deal, they'll be in a better position to stand up to the big spreads and the cartel."

"Excellently done," Ki complimented her. "What were the final terms?"

"Starbuck Enterprises will furnish the ranchers with second mortgages based on the equity they already have in their spreads," Jessie replied. "The ranchers will use the money to buy breeding stock and weather out their first tough years in the cattle business. They'll pay the Starbuck organization low interest, either in dollars or livestock. In addition, we get a share of the profits when they begin to develop their coal holdings."

"You mean Tang's coal holdings," Ki smiled. "The other ranchers are getting what amounts to an interest-free loan."

"I can afford it," Jessie shrugged, a grin spreading across her lovely face. "Tang didn't mind giving his friends and neighbors a bit of a free ride, and neither do I. They'll need each other's help—even with the money—to stand up to the rustlers being backed by the larger spreads and the cartel. The important thing is to give them a fighting chance, and to keep the profits from the coal in America, where they belong, and not let them fall into the hands of the Prussians who murdered my father." Jessie paused. "Tang and his neighbors are good, hard workers. Wyoming needs them."

Ki, thinking of a certain widow lady, could only nod.

"The papers will be signed tomorrow afternoon," Jessie added.

"And tonight?" the samurai asked.

"Tonight you and I are guests at Hiram Tang's ranch." Jessie said. "I've got my camp and my horse just on the other side of this ridge. We can light a fire and make some breakfast. Have you eaten?"

"I'm not hungry," Ki began.

"Oh, I know that shrug," Jessie cut him off, scolding him goodnaturedly. "I bet you've neglected to eat for days, am I right?"

Ki could only blush. "It slipped my mind," he said bashfully, taking off his Stetson, to flip back the inky black hair that had fallen across his brow.

"Well, first we eat, because *I'm* hungry," Jessie declared. "Lord above, a girl could waste away to nothing, timing her meals to the likes of you."

"Perhaps a fire is not wise," Ki said slowly. "The rustlers could be in the area."

"Then they'll just have to smell our bacon frying and weep," Jessie replied adamantly. "After breakfast we'll start our ride to Tang's spread."

Ki fought back his grin. "Breakfast it is," he said.

★

Chapter 3

The mesas dwindled in size behind Jessie and Ki. They'd just reached Hiram Tang's staked-out land when the two heard the shots. There were not just one or two reports, which might signify a hunter, but a steady, rattling series, like dry kindling crackling in some gigantic campfire.

"That could be Hiram up against those cow thieves," Jessie worried. "He told me yesterday that he'd taken to patrolling his land. He said he'd been losing too many cattle to those outlaws."

They kneed their mounts into a hard run, and rode over a meadowed rise, to come to a series of granite outcroppings that turned the trail into a maze. Gray clouds of gunsmoke and the stink of spent powder hung in the still, cool air.

"There's Hiram!" Jessie exclaimed, pointing to a man standing behind one of the boulders. He had his rifle steadied on top of the rock, and was firing as fast as he could lever rounds into his weapon's chamber.

From their vantage point on the rise, Jessie and Ki could see what Hiram was shooting at. The rustlers had set up a makeshift camp in a clearing about fifty yards from where Hiram was making his stand. Ten yards in front of the rancher's boulder lay a horse. It was a bay mare, its side ripped open by rifle bullets. One leg kicked feebly in the air.

"We've got to help him!" Jessie cried out. She'd already drawn her Winchester out of its saddle boot.

Before she could ride off, Ki grabbed hold of her mount's reins. Her tan gelding, confused by the contradictory commands and already very frightened by the noise of the battle down below, showed the whites of its eyes as it snorted and bucked.

"What are you up to?" Jessie demanded of Ki as she struggled to bring her mount back under her control. The animal quieted to stand trembling and pawing at the ground. "We've got to get down there and lend a hand!"

"Listen to me," Ki ordered sternly. "Our horses are not army mounts. They're not accustomed to gunfire. It won't help us to have those rustlers shoot our mounts the way they shot Hiram Tang's."

Jessie nodded meekly. "You're right, of course. What should we do?"

Ki had already drawn his Japanese bow, a strangely warped-looking, crookedly shaped weapon, about four feet long. "I want you to tether our mounts in that stand of aspens we passed on the far side of the rise. There they will be safe and calm." He strapped his quiver of arrows about his waist, resting it behind his left hip, and quickly dismounted. "Once that is done, join us down below, but be careful!"

As Jessie led their horses back over the rise's summit, Ki scurried down to join the badly outnumbered rancher. The rustlers were not returning Tang's fire. Ki considered that a bad omen. It meant that the cow thieves were professionals who were not easily panicked. Most likely they were waiting for the rancher to use up all of his ammunition. Then they could attack with no risk to themselves.

Tang whirled around as Ki approached. "Who the hell

are you?" the frightened rancher gasped, trying to bring his Winchester around to cover the newcomer.

Ki was close enough to grab the rifle's hot barrel. He wrenched it easily from Tang's grasp. "I am a friend," the samurai assured the man. "I am here with Jessica Starbuck. She will join us shortly."

"All right, all right," Tang muttered. "You're that Japanese fellow she mentioned." Tang was a gaunt, red-haired man of medium height, dressed in baggy denim pants and a faded red and black plaid wool shirt. He did not wear a handgun, but the bellows pockets of his shirt bulged with what Ki assumed were extra cartridges for his old .44-40 Winchester.

Ki handed the man back his rifle. As if that were his cue, Tang went immediately back to firing toward the rustlers' camp.

"Save your ammunition," Ki said. "You do not have any targets but rocks just now."

"I know that, dammit!" Tang scowled. "I'm trying to force them into playing their hand."

"The way to do that is not to fire," Ki said mildly. "Once they realize that you are going to force them into making the next move, they will make it."

Just then, Jessie joined the two men. She had her own Winchester in her hand, and her saddlebags over her shoulder. "Extra rounds," she said, tapping the bags. "And a couple of canteens."

"I sure could use a drink of water," Tang murmured, licking his dry lips. Jessie handed him one of the canteens, and he took several long swallows.

"What happened?" she asked as Tang handed the canteen back to her. "How'd you get yourself into this mess, Hiram?"

"I was riding my land when I came upon them," Tang began. "I was coming from that direction," he pointed with his rifle toward the rustlers. "I found myself in the midst of their camp before I knew what was happening. There's ten of them over yonder, and they've got twenty-odd head of my cattle in a rope corral. That fire there is so they can heat up their branding irons. They mean to change my mark."

"How is that done?" Ki asked. "It seems to me that it would be obvious if a man's brand were changed."

"Not at all, friend," Tang muttered. "Easiest thing in the world. Now, my brand is the Triple D." He crouched down and drew **DDD** into the dirt with the point of a twig. "That brand is registered with the government as mine."

"Could they merely deface it and get away with that?" Ki wondered.

"But they don't deface it," Tang glowered. "They change it! Here, look." He picked up his twig. "Say those thieves are carrying a running iron that makes the 'rocker' mark." He drew a curve, like a smile, or the single runner of a rocking chair, into the dirt. "All they have to do is brand that mark beneath my Triple D to make it the *Rocking* Triple D." He threw the twig away in disgust.

"But what about ownership papers?" Ki asked.

Tang chuckled. "In this territory, the brand is what counts, friend. Papers are even easier to fake. Hell, a lot of folks out here can't even read!"

From the rustlers' encampment came the sound of a rifle shot. The round ricocheted off the boulder the three were crouched behind, dusting them with pulverized granite.

"Looks like you were right," Tang smiled at Ki.

"Hiram, you really shouldn't have tried to stand them off by yourself," Jessie scolded.

"I've got to say that this wasn't my plan," the rancher admitted sheepishly. "Like I told you, I rode right into them before I knew it. I didn't stop, but before I could ride out of range they shot my horse out from under me. I grabbed my rifle and scrambled behind this here rock. It's been a Mexican standoff ever since."

"They could just ride off," Ki offered.

"They could," Jessie said, shaking her head, "but they won't. Hiram caught them with their irons in that fire, right out there in the open. If they pulled back, they'd have to leave those irons—"

Jessie's words were drowned out by gunfire erupting from the rustlers' campsite. Rounds struck their boulder and whined off. Hiram Tang ducked down out of sight while Jessie and Ki took up positions on either side of the rock. One of the rustlers made a zigzag run for the campfire, firing his pistol as he did so. The other cow thieves kept up their rifle and revolver fire, trying to cover their man.

Jessie levered a round into her Winchester and sighted down on the runner. She squeezed the trigger just as the man reached the campfire. As the rifle butt thudded against her shoulder, she saw the rustler clutch at his neck and spin to the ground.

"As I was saying," Jessie said, levering a fresh cartridge into her rifle, "they can't leave those running irons sitting in that fire. All along, it's been the larger spreads' contention that there are no rustlers plaguing the smaller ranchers."

"I get it!" Tang interrupted eagerly. "If we got ahold of those running irons, we'd have proof that there's cow thieves around. It'd no longer be just our word against the big spreads'!"

"It is still nine of them against three of us," Ki remarked. "And we cannot count on a repetition of that last desperate ploy on their part."

"He sure talks funny," Tang whispered to Jessie.

"I suspect that they are already spreading out among these rocks," Ki continued, causing Tang and Jessie to look about them uneasily. "Jessie, you must get away."

"Now just a minute, Ki!" Jessie hotly began to argue. "This is no time for us to split up!"

"It is precisely the time," Ki cut her off, his calm, even tone overriding Jessie's emotional outburst. "You must ride to Nettle Grove for help."

"That's over three hours from here!" Jessie exclaimed, her green eyes flashing. "Six hours there and back. You two can't hold out that long."

"We've got no choice," Tang said. "I agree with your friend. Maybe they'll give it up and leave without those running irons. Hell, they'll be able to see you getting away, but by then you'll be out of rifle range. Knowing that they've got a time limit—even if it is a six-hour one—might just spook them into running."

Jessie glanced skeptically at the two men. "Don't tell me you both believe that."

"Somebody has got to go for help," Ki said.

"Then it ought to be Hiram," Jessie said.

"No way," Tang glowered.

"Hiram Tang, I'm a better shot than you are, and you know it!" Jessie argued.

"Might be, but I'm not leaving a woman behind while I ride off," the rancher insisted stubbornly. "So you're going."

"That's—"

"Jessie," Ki broke in, "there is another, perhaps more unpleasant reason, but one we must face. If the rustlers should overrun us, you must survive. Both Tang and I can be sacrificed, but if you were to be killed, the cartel would win."

Ki's argument struck home. Jessie pondered it, but there was not getting around the fact that what the samurai said was true. "I'll leave the canteens and extra rounds," she murmured.

"Take both horses," Ki ordered. "Switch from one to the other. You'll make better time."

"We could all go!" Jessie said hopefully.

Ki shook his head. "Three of us on only two horses? They would catch us for sure. And what of the running irons? Go on, Jessie."

She stared into Ki's eyes. "See you soon," she whispered.

Ki smiled at her. "Soon," he agreed.

"Get a move on, girl," Tang growled. He peeked over the top of the boulder, his Winchester at the ready. "No telling where those thieves are. The longer you wait, the more risk you'll be taking until you reach your horses."

Jessie sprinted off, her rifle at the ready. Ki did not look back, but concentrated on scanning the area before him. He drew an arrow from his lacquered quiver, and nocked it into his bowstring. "Hiram, let me know when she has gotten out of their range," he muttered quietly.

"I will," the rancher said. "I don't know why you didn't ask for her rifle. Two rifles against eight would have been bad enough. But now it's only one rifle and some damned peculiar-looking arrows. What the hell kind of arrowhead *is* that, anyway?"

"This is one of twenty-four different types of war arrows," Ki explained. "The twenty-four are called *nakazashi*. I've chosen the arrow called the 'belly-cutter.'"

At first, Tang was puzzled, but as he stared at the twisting, corkscrew shape of the arrowhead, the meaning of its name became clear to him. "You shoot that thing into a man's belly?" he asked, and when Ki nodded, the rancher shuddered, saying, "If you ask me, it's a hell of a lot more neighborly to plug a fellow with a good old .44."

"Is she safely away?" Ki asked.

Tang peered over his shoulder. "Yep. She's over the ridge."

Ki nodded in satisfaction. "I am going into that boulder-studded area between ourselves and the enemy. If I keep my head down, I will not be seen by any of the rustlers maneuvering to surround us. Or at least I won't be seen until it is too late for the sight of me to do them any good," the samurai added. "It will be myself against them in a maze, and the advantage will be mine, for I can kill anything I come across, while they will first have to ascertain whether their target is friend or foe."

"Uh, right," Tang nodded, his eyes still on the glistening tip of the "belly-cutter" arrow. "What do you want me to do?"

Ki thought about that. He was uneasy with Tang as his only ally. Oh, the man was a decent enough fellow, and Ki was certain he was a good rancher. However, Tang seemed to lack a warrior's skills. The man fired when he should not, and tended to hug the ground when it was time to strike. Ki did not consider Tang a coward, but simply one of the multitude who waged all their battles in their daydreams.

"You can be of greatest service by staying right here," the samurai began. "If you should get a shot at any of them, take it, but under no account should you expose yourself to their fire."

"'Course not," Tang grumbled. "What kind of fool do you take me for?"

"I meant that you should not be taken in by any of their ruses," Ki explained. He stared at Tang, and sighed. There was no time to give the man lessons in strategy. "Good luck," he muttered, and slipped away toward the rustlers' encampment.

It was, indeed, like a maze. As long as he kept himself lower than the tops of the many boulders in the field, he could hunt in relative safety. He kept his bow at the ready, which was a fortunate thing, for he met his first outlaw head-on.

The man was crouched fifteen feet away. The only thing that gave Ki an edge was the fact that the man was armed with a rifle instead of a pistol. The extra time it took the outlaw to swing the longer firearm in Ki's direction was all the time the samurai needed. Ki pulled back on the bowstring and let the shaft fly. It hissed across the five-yard distance to puncture the outlaw's stomach. The man cried out, dropping his rifle and toppling forward on his knees. His fall forced the arrow's shaft deeper into his body. The corkscrew point ripped through the man's back, tearing a jagged hole through his jacket.

The rustler's death cry would attract others to the scene. Ki fitted another arrow to his bowstring and waited. This shaft had a traditional arrow head, but a ceramic bulb was fitted just aft of its business end. Holes in the bulb were designed to catch the wind as the arrow flew.

Ki let it fly at the first outlaw to reveal himself, a man about twenty yards away. The air rushing through the bulb created a high-pitched keening sound. The rustler looked sideways and up at the sky, his revolver wavering uncertainly. He was still trying to figure out what the noise was, and where it was coming from, when the "death's song" arrow took him through the neck.

Ki did not wait to watch his target fall. He slipped away, weaving between the boulders the way a trout weaves its way along the bottom of a lake.

"What the hell was that noise?" Ki heard one of the outlaws call nervously to another. "Some kind of bird?"

"Jack's dead!" hissed a new voice coming from a different direction. "He's been hit with a arrow!"

"What are we up against? Indians?"

"These ain't Ute arrows, I can tell you that!"

Ki kept moving back toward where he'd left Tang, and away from those gathered voices. There were now too many of them in one place. It was better to bide his time. Ki was beginning to think they were going to get out of this alive. Tang was showing admirable sense—

Ki literally bumped into one of the rustlers. The man grabbed Ki's bow at the same time that the samurai locked his fingers about the wrist of the outlaw's gun hand.

"I got him!" shouted the rustler. He was a big, strong man, and knew how to wrestle. He lurched backward, planting his boots against Ki's chest as he did so. The samurai's bow fell as he was propelled forward and up into the air by the rustler's jackknifing legs. *No time for this,* Ki thought desperately as he somersaulted over the cow thief's head, to land jarringly upon the ground.

Throughout his fall, Ki had held on to the man's wrist, immobilizing it so that the rustler could not aim his pistol. Now Ki executed a wrist-twist that caused the revolver to slip from the rustler's fingers. Ki flipped over on his belly and swatted the gun away with the back of his hand. The pistol was out of reach, but Ki's sending it there had given his adversary time to rise up on his knees and twist around, getting behind the samurai. The man locked his thick forearm across Ki's windpipe.

The two struggled like that, on their knees, for some seconds. Ki had to drive his elbow into the man's rock-hard belly three times before the cow thief's choke-hold loosened. A shot ricocheted off granite, sending stinging chips of stone against Ki's cheek as he wrenched free of the other man's grasp.

"Hurry up!" the rustler groaned, looking past Ki, and rubbing at his bruised belly. He pulled a hunting knife from its sheath on his gunbelt, and rushed toward the samurai.

Ki faltered as he reached for a *shuriken* blade, his intentions forgotten as he watched Hiram Tang leave his cover to charge toward the struggle. The rancher was firing his Winchester from the hip, aiming merely to hold off the other rustlers from shooting Ki in the back.

"Hiram! Find cover!" Ki cried out, and then there was no time to find his own blade, for the rustler's long knife was being thrust toward his gut. Ki sidestepped to the left, beginning to counter the man's knife attack with a *gedan-barai,* or downward block. As Ki moved sideways, he brought his right fist up across his own chest. Then, as the rustler extended his knife hand, Ki snapped his fist downward and to the right, to catch the outside of the rustler's hand. The cow thief's blade was deflected, and Ki countered with a forward snap-kick to the man's solar plexus, causing his opponent to double over, the wind knocked out of him.

Ki had no time to finish the fellow off. Now that the rustler had fallen away, his companions could open fire. The air was filled with the whine of lead ricocheting off rock. Ki leaped into the air, now resembling a trout on a hook as he twisted and arced his body in an attempt to make himself a more difficult target. The foolhardy but gloriously brave Hiram Tang was still standing out in the open, steadfast and still, as if his boots had rooted to the earth. Fire and blue smoke were pouring from the barrel of his Winchester.

Ki was still in the upward part of his leap. He was attempting to somersault backward and in that way travel over the boulder behind him, putting it between himself and the rustlers pegging shots at him from behind their cover, about ten yards away. At this point they were not even trying for Hiram, even though his fire was pinning them down.

Then Ki saw why that was. One of the rustlers had circled around behind Tang. Ki watched him raise his pistol to shoot the rancher in the back. There was no time for Ki to throw a *shuriken* blade, no time to do anything but watch helplessly as the rustler fired twice, his bullets slamming into Tang and driving him forward, to fall facedown on the ground.

"No!" Ki howled. The concentration essential to execute the difficult backward flip successfully was shattered. He came down too short, to slam his spine across the curved top of the boulder. He slid limply down, collapsing to the ground on the *near* side of the big rock. His legs felt like rubber as he lifted himself purely on the strength of his will—a *samurai's* will—raging at himself to *move*, while his back protested in pain.

The rustlers came around from the rocks they'd been hiding behind, and rushed toward Ki. The samurai counted five of them, and all were firing their guns. Even as he reached for his *shuriken* throwing blades, he knew it was pointless. There were too many.

Then the world flashed as bright and white as the noon summer sun. The sound of gunfire faded abruptly, to be replaced by a deafening noise that was both a roar and a whine. *The sound of my own death rushing toward me,* Ki thought briefly as he felt himself falling from what seemed to be a very great height.

As he lay still, he heard one of the rustlers say quite clearly, "Shoot a man in the head and he bleeds like a stuck pig . . ."

"He's finished," another said jovially.

There was the terrible sound of a pistol's hammer being cocked. Ki, in his fast-growing delirium, thought it was the metallic clang of the bells rung in the temples of his homeland. *Bells being rung to mark his death.*

A rustler crouched down over the samurai. "Hell, he ain't breathing," the man muttered, then added in distaste, "His head's a mess."

"No time to waste," a new voice, one strong with command, now interrupted. "We got bodies of our own boys to gather up, and Christ! Don't forget those damned running irons in the fire. Move it! There's been enough gunshots to restart the Civil War. Somebody might have heard."

Hands were stripping Ki of his arrow quiver, vest, and boots. A voice said, "Get his bow as well. The old man said the girl had a Chinaman on her side. He'll want proof the chink's dead."

"Too bad the girl got away."

"Who cares about her? With this Chinaman dead, we've pulled the hellcat's claws and teeth!"

Ki heard laughter and then, dimly, the sound of bootsteps fading away. He used his last bit of will to control the surge of air rushing from his aching lungs. They must not hear him—

The blinding white light deepened into a pulsating crimson, and then dimmed to blackness. The roaring, whining noise grew in Ki's ears. It sounded like a train barreling toward him along rusty tracks.

As he faded into unconsciousness, he thought of Jessie. He'd failed her by dying. Now she would be alone.

And then even his thinking ceased to be.

Chapter 4

It was pain that had sent Ki into unconsciousness, and it was pain that brought him back to the world. All he had wanted was to be able to go on sleeping—for slumber seemed to the samurai to be an endless, easy ocean in which he had been floating. It would have been a fine thing to go on sleeping, but the swelling, throbbing pain in his head would not permit that.

Ki opened his eyes. It was night. There were no moon or stars, and an odd, faintly glowing fog seemed to cover the ground. He could just make out the darker shadows that were the boulders—

Fog? Ki thought distractedly. *How could there be fog so far from any sea?*

"Stare all you want to at me, Injun," said a boyish voice. "Just don't you try nothing. I know how to use this here rifle."

Ki wondered how the boy could tell he'd been staring in this darkness. Why didn't the boy light a campfire? Then it came to Ki. The realization rose up through the throbbing pain the way an earthworm burrows up through moist loam. The rustlers must still be nearby! Of course! The boy didn't dare build a fire that might give away their presence—

"How close to us are they?" he quietly asked.

"Who?" the boy replied, plainly puzzled.

"The cattle thieves," Ki muttered.

"Them!" The boy swore softly. "Beats me, Injun. I reckon they're long gone, though."

Then why no campfire? Ki wondered. "Who are you?"

The shadowy form moved off to blend into the general darkness. A few moments later it returned. Then Ki felt cool water spill across his mouth.

"Drink, Injun!" the boy demanded impatiently. "My name's Danny Tang."

Ki pushed the canteen away from his mouth. "Danny," he whispered. "You are Hiram's son?"

"You got it right, Injun."

"I am sorry about your father, Danny," Ki said.

"Well, I aim to make those cow thieves a lot sorrier!" the boy vowed fiercely. "At first I thought you was one of them. I swear, I almost pumped a bullet into you to finish you off."

"Danny, please believe me," Ki began. "I am not one of them."

"I know *that,*" the boy interrupted. "I figured that out myself," he added proudly. "I prowled around, found some bloody puddles in the dirt. That told me my pa had gotten a few of them. Well, if they took their other dead, why would they have left one of their *wounded* behind? Anyhow, I never heard of white men—law-abiding or otherwise—riding with a half-breed Injun."

"I was fighting with your father, not against him," Ki muttered through clenched teeth as the pain suddenly grew to fill his entire head. "Is—is your father dead?"

"Yeah," the boy said, his voice overly flat, as if he were trying to deny the note of trembling Ki had heard. "My pa's dead. How'd it happen?"

"They shot him just before they shot me—"

"You ain't shot," Danny cut him off. "Leastways, not in the usual sense of the word. As near as I can figure it, a ricochet, or a chip of rock splintered off by a ricocheting slug, hit you right good and proper along the left side of your head. You got a big open cut traveling along just above your eye. There was a lot of blood," the boy added matter-of-factly. "Lucky for you, those outlaws were in a hurry. It was all that blood on your face that fooled them. I washed it off and bandaged up your head as best I could. Had to tear up your shirt, sort of, to make the bandages..."

"A head wound," Ki muttered thickly. "A concussion..."

"What's that? What'd you say, Injun?" Danny asked sharply. "Speak up. Stay awake! You're fading away! You can sleep when I leave."

Leave? Ki thought. Where could the boy go at night? Jessie, Ki remembered. If it was night, she had most certainly reached Nettle Grove—and had by now returned to the site of the battle.

"Hello?" the boy nudged him.

"Danny, listen to me," Ki said, relieved. "There are people looking for us. To help us. Back where you found me and your father—"

"What?" the boy asked disgustedly. "Stop your yapping. I think that head graze of yours has addled your fool Injun brains. You want something to yap about, try this on for size. Those rustlers took all your stuff," he taunted. "Your gun and boots and horse." He snickered. "Don't know why, Injun."

"Please, you must listen!" Ki pleaded weakly for the boy's attention. It was becoming ever more difficult to talk. He wanted so much to sleep... "We must return to the place where you found me."

"What are you talking about?" the boy chuckled, amused by what he took to be delirious ramblings. "Go *where?*"

"Where you found me," Ki gasped. The pain was splitting his skull.

"We *are* where I found you! Hell, my pa's lying right over there—" The boy stopped abruptly, having shocked himself by momentarily forgetting, and then *remembering*, what had happened to his father.

Ki paused, confused. Surely Jessie would have returned by now, he thought. It was night. But a moonless night! That was it! It was so dark that she could not lead the rescue party to the correct location.

"Danny, you must build a fire," Ki began.

"What?" the boy muttered distractedly, and then laughed. "You *are* addled, Injun. Why would I want to build a fire?"

"The rescue party. With no moon, it is too dark. A fire will be a beacon to lead them to us."

The boy did not answer immediately. Ki peered at his silent, shadowy silhouette. "Danny?"

"I'm here," the boy said quickly. The amusement seemed to have left his voice. "The dark, you say?"

"Yes, the night—"

"Mister, it ain't night. It ain't even three o'clock in the afternoon," Danny said in hushed tones. "The sun's overhead, shining bright as can be."

"Sun shining . . ." Ki repeated thickly. He tried to sit up, but that only increased his pain and brought on an overwhelming wave of dizziness. He stayed flat on his back, gingerly exploring his face and head. The bandages only covered his forehead. There was nothing across his eyes . . .

He stared up into the dark, evening heavens that this boy said were sunny skies. "You are a liar!" Ki began to rage, but then stopped. His whole body stiffened as he realized how *warm* it was. Where were the cool Wyoming night breezes? What could this warmth be but the sun beating down on him, bathing his face?

The sun beating down upon a black-fog world peopled by shadows. His new world . . .

"Danny?" Ki heard—and was instantly ashamed of—the womanly note of hysteria in his voice.

"I gotta go, mister," the boy said shakily. "I've got things to do . . ."

Ki watched the blur that was Danny moving off. It faded into the general blackness. "Danny?" Ki used all the courage he could muster in trying to keep his voice calm and manly.

"You said you had friends coming," Danny said, from so close by that Ki started. "You meant that, right?"

Ki ignored him. "I am blind," he whispered.

"Mister?"

Ki heard no more. The pain in his head had combined with the despair, as thick and black as bile, that was swelling in the pit of his stomach. He could not see the world, and as if to mock him, the world was now spinning around. Then it was Ki himself who was spinning, back into the oblivion of sleep, where he had no need for his useless eyes.

★

Chapter 5

Nettle Grove's town marshal kept Jessie waiting. She'd cooled her heels sitting on the plank bench outside his office for over an hour. While she sat, watching the township's citizens ambling along Main Street, she kept worrying about how Ki and Hiram Tang were faring against those killers. It had occurred to her during her long, hard ride to Nettle Grove that Ki would have stood a better chance *alone*. Being saddled with Hiram Tang could only slow him down.

When she was finally allowed inside the marshal's office, having been summoned by a deputy, she tried to launch right into her story. Before she could, the marshal stopped her with an idle wave of his hand.

"With you in a moment," he mumbled, not even lifting his eyes from the papers on his desk. "Just got to finish reading this here report."

Jessie looked around the room, fighting to keep her temper under control. A door to the rear, behind the marshal's desk, led to the jail cells. Along one wall was a rack of rifles and shotguns. Beneath the rack, facing the wall, was another desk. There, the blond-haired young deputy who had summoned her sat with his back to the room, scribbling away with a steel-nibbed pen, working on what was probably yet another report for the marshal.

On the wall opposite the gun rack hung a colorful if tattered collection of wanted posters, and a duty roster showing when each deputy was supposed to be on patrol. There were several straight-backed chairs in the middle of the office, but right now, Jessie was too anxious to sit.

"Marshal Forbes," Jessie icily addressed the man, unable to hold back any longer. "I informed you that this was an emergency, that men's lives were at stake. Is this how you—"

"Just simmer down, young lady," the town marshal smirked. He pushed aside his papers. "Tempest in a teapot, I'll bet. All you women are alike." The marshal was a short, potbellied man about forty years old. His nose was red-veined, and he had a series of flabby chins that dwindled away toward the collar of his red wool shirt. He was totally bald on top and wore what hair he had left in an oily, dark, horseshoe fringe. He had a brass star pinned to his right shirt pocket flap, and an old, battered Colt .45 riding beneath his left armpit, in a shoulder holster.

"Now then, Miss Starbuck," the marshal grinned as he leaned back in his swivel chair and propped his feet up on his battered-looking oak desk. "You've been stirring things up hotter then a hornet's nest since you arrived in Nettle Grove. Today you run in here with a new tale about how the sky is falling. You can't expect me to jump up and leave everything just because a pretty little thing like you *says* there's some sort of emergency—"

"Now you listen to me, Forbes," Jessie seethed.

"No!" Forbes slammed his palm down upon his desk to cut her off. "You listen to me, because *I'm* the town marshal here, and because the name Starbuck don't cut no mustard in *these* parts."

"Forbes—"

"You'll address me as 'marshal,' little miss," he warned. "Else I just might teach you the manners your daddy never did!"

You try, and you'll catch a bullet in that pot belly of yours, Jessie thought, but did not say so out loud. If she was going to get anywhere with this fool, she would have to dance to his tune. She took a deep breath, trying to tame her fury. "I apologize, Marshal Forbes. May I tell you what's happened?"

"That's better, Miss Starbuck," Forbes said gloatingly. "You just go right ahead."

Calmly and coherently, Jessie recounted the events of the morning, beginning at the point when she and Ki had heard Hiram Tang's shots. She spoke in flat declarative sentences, leaving nothing out, including the fact that she herself had shot and most likely killed one of the outlaws. She even did her best to ignore Forbes's snort of disbelief at that last fact. As she told her story, Jessie was aware that the deputy had stopped his deskwork in order to listen in. As Jessie spoke, she began to feel a new surge of hope. Nothing in what she was saying—or in how she was saying it—could give these two men grounds to dismiss her tale as the delusions of a hysterical woman.

Forbes had listened patiently. "You done?" he finally asked, and when Jessie nodded, the town marshal chuckled quietly, shaking his head.

"I swear Miss Starbuck, you should have been in the theater. You're pretty enough, what with that long, yellow-red hair of yours, and those green eyes. And you've got a fine figure," he observed. "Normally I don't hold with women wearing trousers, but they do suit you, I've got to say—"

"What is your point, Marshal?" Jessie demanded, fairly stamping her foot in frustration.

"My point, miss, is that this ain't the stage, and that I don't believe your performance. Even if I did, an educated businesswoman like yourself ought to know that as town marshal, my jurisdiction ends with Nettle Grove's city limits." Forbes shrugged easily. "Now, if I *did* believe you, I might mosey out to where you said all of this shooting took place, just to have me an unofficial look around, but I don't believe you, so it don't matter one way or the other."

Control yourself, Jessie thought. "Marshal, why would I make something like this up?"

"I'll answer that with a question of my own," Forbes smiled. He was clearly having a grand old time playing cat-and-mouse. "You know what a carpetbagger is?"

Jessie was momentarily taken back. "What are you *talking* about?"

"Carpetbaggers was folks who came South from up North to reap the profits that fairly belonged to others," Forbes scowled. "Oh, I know they had *official* duties," he spat. "But we all know what they were really there for—to skim the cream off the milk *other* folks had tugged out of the cow."

"Is that what you think of me, Marshal?" Jessie asked.

"Yes, miss, I do." Forbes nodded. "We were all doing mighty fine in Nettle Grove and hereabouts, and then you came, and before you, these new, so-called cattlemen showed up. Now these new, smaller ranchers aren't bad fellows, I'll give them that," the marshal said shrewdly. "But they've come too late. The territory hereabouts has all been spoken for by the cattlemen who made Wyoming Territory desirable in the first place."

"But men like Hiram Tang have settled on rangeland nobody else wanted!" Jessie argued.

Forbes shrugged. "Well, now somebody else *does* want it."

"You mean Tom Schiff, don't you, Marshal?" Jessie smiled thinly.

"I do, miss," Forbes declared. "Tom's Lazy C outfit is the biggest in Wyoming. Why, his contributions helped build this town, and it's his money—"

"That pays your salary?" Jessie asked sarcastically.

Forbes's eyes narrowed. "You be right careful now, little miss, else you might be the one who ends up locked up. What I was going to say is that it's Tom's bank that does the money-lending around here. We got no need for Starbuck money."

"*You* don't, but men like Hiram Tang do," Jessie countered. "And I intend to lend it to them. That's not carpetbagging, Marshal." She shook her head. "Just because I aim to do something that's not to Tom Schiff's liking doesn't make it illegal."

"It makes it mighty unpopular, dammit!" Forbes growled, and then, to Jessie's surprise, blushed. "Didn't mean to swear, miss... Look, Miss Starbuck. I know you don't think much of me, but you can count on the fact that if anything was to happen to you, I'd do my best to find the man that did it, even if it was Tom Schiff. The point is, you'd already be dead, or *worse*. That's what I meant about your activities in Nettle Grove being unpopular."

"If you say so, Marshal," Jessie nodded evenly. "But I still don't understand why you think I'd make up a story about rustlers. Why, Hiram Tang and the other ranchers—"

"I call them land grabbers," Forbes sullenly cut her off.

"What?"

"Land grabbers," Forbes repeated adamantly. "Hiram Tang and his friends are land grabbers, trying to grab what already should belong to Tom Schiff by dint of all he's done for the territory. And I think that you and Hiram Tang would make up this rustler stuff to give you a reason to go stirring up the other small ranchers. Admit it! You and Tang want to organize some newfangled cattlemen's association, to spoil the one that Tom's established."

"Marshal, it's clear that you and I can never see eye-to-eye on this," Jessie sighed. "You call Hiram Tang a land grabber, and I say the same thing about Tom Schiff." She was about to say more, but gave it up. What good could it do to tell what she'd learned about the coal deposits, or about the fact that Schiff was in league with the Prussians?

Forbes would just laugh off those allegations as well. She sighed. "It's plain to me that I'm wasting my time with you, Marshal."

"That's the first thing we can agree on, miss," Forbes said by way of dismissal.

"I want you to know that I intend to wire the sheriff at Cough Creek, and the federal marshal's office in Denver," she announced.

"I don't care what you do," Forbes muttered. "You, Tang, or your chink boyfriend—as long as it isn't against the law."

Jessie felt the marshal's eyes drilling twin holes in her back as she stormed out of the office. Just as she was closing the door she heard him say to his deputy, "Hank, watch over things for a bit. I'm going over to the bank."

More than likely to have a little parley with Tom Schiff, Jessie thought glumly. How foolish she'd been to think that the law would be even-handed, here in Schiff's town!

The telegraph office was down by the railroad station. As she hurried along Main Street's raised wooden sidewalks, past the stores, saloons, and cafes, she wondered what her plan of action ought to be after she'd sent her wire. She'd failed in getting Forbes to raise a posse, and there was no other law in the vicinity. The only folks she could turn to for help were Tang's peers, the smaller ranch owners. The problem was, it would take the rest of the day just to ride to all of their spreads to notify them. Once that was accomplished, who was to say how many of them could leave their ranches? Most of the smaller operations were family-run.

Jessie turned right at the corner where Main Street intersected with a narrow avenue dubbed Schiff Street. Forbes was right, this *was* Tom Schiff's town. Here the raised sidewalks ended, and rows of whitewashed clapboard houses began. Jessie passed a grammar school that was just letting out for the afternoon. A small one-story building adjacent to the school proudly proclaimed itself as the Nettle Grove Public Library.

Behind the library were some railroad warehouses, and behind those were the holding pens and loading ramps for cattle going East. Jessie crossed the railroad tracks to the telegraph office, which was huddled behind the station depot. It was little more than a shack, and if Jessie hadn't known better, she would have mistaken the telegraph office for a baggage shed.

The clerk behind the counter was a pink-cheeked teenager who looked like he still had no need of a razor. He wore a white shirt buttoned to the throat, a dark blue cap with a brass stamping across the front that read WESTERN UNION, and a big, happy, absurdly sexual grin as he leered at Jessie.

"What can I do for *you?*" the boy asked, his voice full of spunk, his eyes riveted on Jessie's breasts outlined beneath the white silk of her blouse.

"You can calm down, for one thing," Jessie said, amused. "We wouldn't want you to stunt your growth."

The boy swallowed hard and blushed a bright tomato red. "Um, sorry, ma'am," he said docilely. "Please don't report me to the home office. I—"

"I'd like to send a telegram," Jessie said, taking pity on the kid. "As for your behavior when I entered, I take that as a compliment from a young gentleman." She opened her big green eyes wide, and smiled at the clerk. "Wasn't that how you meant it?"

"Yes, ma'am!" the boy gulped, practically melting beneath Jessie's warm gaze. He stared, lovestruck, for a moment, and then once more blushed himself back to his senses at Jessie's silvery laugh.

Jessie took the proffered blank of yellow flimsy and the pencil, and went off into a corner of the office to compose her message. She'd already decided to send only one telegram—not to the sheriff in Cough Creek, or the Denver federal marshal's office, but to her own Starbuck office in Denver. Wyoming was only a territory. Denver was the nearest big city. Jessie was willing to wager that the agreements between Tom Schiff and the cartel were drawn up and signed in Denver. She would instruct her office to do their utmost to find proof of Schiff's association with the Prussians. It wouldn't be enough to incriminate the cattle baron, even if her Denver people did find some shred of evidence, but it was a start. You got a little piece here and a little piece there, and before you knew it, the picture came together. Such evidence would certainly help her to present a more solid case to Forbes, especially if Ki and Hiram Tang had managed to get the rustlers' running irons.

She also asked her office to inform both the Cough Creek sheriff and the marshal's office in Denver of the rustler problem, but Jessie did not expect help from either quarter. Cattle rustling was low on the list of priorities that might make a county sheriff or U.S. marshal come running. That was especially true when it was a bunch of uninfluential smaller ranchers who were being victimized.

She handed the filled-out blank to the clerk. He scanned its length and said, "You could save yourself a bit of money by sending this as a night wire instead of a straight telegram."

"Send it straightaway," Jessie replied. "Thanks for the tip, but I'd rather not lose a day."

She paid the young clerk and turned to go, but found her way blocked by Marshal Forbes. Behind the lawman was another man who could only be Tom Schiff himself.

"Don't send that just yet, Jeff," Schiff called out to the young clerk.

"I believe it's against the law for someone to interfere with Western Union," Jessie addressed Marshal Forbes.

"Uh, she's right, Tom," Forbes said sheepishly.

"I don't intend to interfere," Schiff grinned. He was a heavyset man in his sixties, but he was tall, and that allowed him to carry his weight well. Schiff was dressed in a dark green corduroy suit, light tan shirt, and black string tie. He wore a flat-topped Stetson with silver conchos set all around his hatband. His Justin boots were polished shiny, and elaborately hand-stitched. "Don't intend that at all," the cattle baron repeated. He removed his mirrored hat to run his hand across his close-cropped head of gray hair. His watery blue eyes, set close together in his ruddy face, narrowed as he stared at the young clerk. "I just wanted to remind Jeff that he was closing early today."

"Closing early, sir?" the boy asked nervously. He glanced apologetically at Jessie.

"No laws against that now, is there, Cal?"

"No, sir," Forbes said. "I guess not," he shrugged, his eyes downcast.

"I just have this one last wire to send, Mr. Schiff," the clerk began.

"I think you better save it for first thing in the morning," Schiff told the young man.

"Don't get yourself into trouble, Jeff," Jessie smiled at the clerk. Turning to Schiff, she said, "Do you really think that keeping me from sending a wire is going to stop me?"

"A little bird told me that you were calling in federal law," Schiff said coldly.

"A potbellied, brass-starred little bird, I bet," Jessie muttered, staring at Forbes. She could tell that the town marshal was uneasy with Schiff's heavy-handed ways, and she wanted to plant a few seeds of guilt and doubt in Forbes.

Schiff shook his head. "We don't need federal law. This here's a nice, peaceful town." He unbuttoned his coat and held it open. "You see, I don't even wear a gun."

"You don't have to," Jessie snapped. She gestured at Forbes. "He wears it for you."

"Now that's enough of your insinuations!" Forbes exploded.

"Easy now, Marshal," soothed a deep, masculine voice coming from behind both Forbes and Schiff.

Jessie looked past the marshal and the cattleman, to see that the deputy named Hank had entered. He was the man who'd been present in the town marshal's office when Jessie had told her story.

"I thought I told you to watch the store," Forbes growled ill-temperedly.

"I thought that maybe you'd want me to take over here,

Marshal," the deputy said in an unruffled, easygoing manner. "That way you could get back to, uh, more important duties."

"Right!" Forbes fairly jumped at the chance to get away. "Thanks, Hank. Uh, I'll be going, Tom, if you don't need me . . ."

"Go right ahead," Schiff nodded, and Forbes hurried away gratefully. "Deputy," Schiff began, "what do you think of a woman sashaying around wearing a gunfighter's rig like that one?" he asked, pointing his finger at Jessie's Colt.

Jessie answered before the deputy could. "I don't like wearing a gun, Mr. Schiff," she declared, and then smiled at the cattle baron. "I also know that a certain sort of man can feel quite frightened and intimidated by the sight." A sideways glance told her that the deputy had been forced to clamp his hand across his face to stifle his appreciative chuckle.

"Me? Afraid of a woman?" Schiff thundered.

"You said it, I didn't," Jessie said sweetly. "In any event, I don't wear this gun unless I think I'm going to have to use it."

"*If* you can use it," Schiff began skeptically, but then froze.

Jessie had drawn her Colt and leveled it at Schiff in the blink of an eye.

"Here now," the deputy began, but before he could say another word, Jessie had her gun reholstered.

"I can use it, Schiff," she said as she stared into the cattleman's face. Spittle had collected in the corners of his thin, bloodless lips. His whole body was shaking with fury. "I can use it, and I did, this morning. You've got one less cow thief on your payroll."

"Be careful, miss," the deputy quietly warned from his corner of the room. "That's a serious accusation to make."

"It's all right. It's all right, Deputy," Schiff said, his voice taut with rage. "Let her talk!"

"You've lost already, Schiff!" Jessie spat, equally as

angry as the cattleman. "Tomorrow morning I'm meeting Hiram Tang right here in your town, and we're signing our partnership papers. It's all over—"

"It's not over until those papers are filled out and signed, Miss Starbuck," Schiff chuckled, seemingly having regained his good humor. "Tomorrow is a long way off!" He was still laughing as he took his leave of the telegraph office.

A moment later the clerk asked, "What should I do about her wire, Deputy?"

The man shrugged. "Reckon you'd better do like Mr. Schiff says, if you want to keep your job."

"Oh!" Jessie seethed. "You're as bad as Forbes!" She stormed out of the office.

The deputy caught up with her outside. He gently took hold of her upper arm to turn her around. "No call for you to insult me," he said softly.

"No?" Jessie asked sarcastically. *"Aren't* you just as bad as Forbes?" Even as she scolded the deputy, she realized that he was quite good looking, in a weatherbeaten, craggy sort of way. He was tall and lean of build, with light brown eyes and a mop of curly yellow hair springing out from underneath his hat.

"No I ain't," the deputy said goodnaturedly. "And old Cal Forbes ain't so bad either. Sure, he may kowtow to Schiff, but Forbes is in nobody's pocket, if you know what I mean."

Jessie shrugged noncommittally. "If you say so," she murmured.

The deputy sighed. "Let's us approach this matter from another direction," he began. "Now, Miss Starbuck, I've got to say that I know a little bit about you since you arrived in our fair township." He grinned, showing a mouthful of strong white teeth. "You hail from Texas, right?"

"Yes," Jessie replied impatiently. "Deputy, I've got things to do—"

"I bet you've got yourself a big old Texas cattle ranch—"

"The Circle Star," Jessie nodded. "It's one of the biggest in the whole Lone Star State!" she proudly proclaimed.

"Knew that it was," the deputy chuckled. "Would there be some sort of town close by?"

"Sarah, Texas," Jessie murmured, beginning to see where this softspoken, clever man was leading her. "My father helped establish it, and they named the town after my mother."

"Uh, yeah," The deputy said, doing his best to keep a straight face. "Now let me ask you something. Supposin' I was to ride into Sarah and start shooting my mouth off about how I was going to cross the Starbucks every which way I could—what do you think would be the first thing the town marshal would do?"

"Chop off your head and send it mounted to me," Jessie said quickly and then laughed.

"Sorry I asked, but I do believe you get my point."

"I do, Deputy," Jessie blushed. "I'm afraid I've been acting very foolishly."

"Well, since you mention it, Miss Starbuck—my name's Hank Stills by the way—since you mention it, I'd say that you're a woman with a hot temper. You let your spirit do your talking and then you do your thinking afterwards. Twice today I've watched you show your cards for no reason. You told poor Marshal Forbes that you were sending for federal law—"

"What was wrong with that, Deputy Stills?"

"Call me Hank," he replied. "What was wrong with it was that you should've known that he was going to run and tell old man Schiff. And just now you went and spilled the beans about signing papers with Hiram Tang tomorrow . . ."

"Enough!" Jessie held up her hands in surrender.

"I don't even want to begin to scold you about throwing around cow-theft charges at the most important man in town."

"I said enough!" Jessie scowled.

"There's that temper again," he groaned, causing Jessie to smile. "Ah, that's better," he drawled. "You're right pretty when you draw that there Colt of yours, but *damn,* you're *beautiful* when you smile."

Jessie regarded the fellow. She knew that deputy town marshals didn't earn very much. This was a fact attested to by Hank Stills's patched, worn jeans, scuffed boots, and old but freshly laundered gray flannel shirt. He wore a red bandanna about his neck and a double-action Colt Model T .44 in his worn, cracked holster. A leather vest, just about as tired-looking as his holster, completed his outfit. The only thing the least bit flashy about the man was the brass star pinned to his vest.

"Tell me something, Hank, what's a smart young n like you doing as a deputy town marshal?"

Stills grinned. "First off, I'm on the other side of thirty— which, I reckon, makes me your elder," he winked. "As for that other stuff all women seem to need to hunt and peck at, I *like* being a lawman. It gives me a lot of time on my own, to think."

"So would being a cattleman," Jessie pointed out. "That pays a lot more, for a lot safer line of work."

The handsome deputy shrugged philosophically. "Maybe so, but money isn't everything. I find upholding the law a darn sight more rewarding than punching cows. And being safe all the time ain't what it's cracked up to be . . ."

Jessie met his friendly gaze. "I know," she murmured.

"I *know* you know," Stills said dryly. "You weren't playing it very safe when you accused Schiff of being a cow thief."

"I didn't!" Jessie pouted. "I said he's got cow thieves on his payroll, but I guess that *is* the same thing."

"You don't have a shred of proof."

"Well, I would," Jessie complained, "if somebody would quit jumping through Schiff's hoops long enough to do the job they were paid to do—" She noticed Stills's frown. "Oh, I'm sorry, Hank. I didn't mean *you.*"

The deputy nodded. He dug a tarnished, dented pocket watch out of his vest and, after looking at it, asked, "You got time for a cup of coffee?"

Jessie gave him a suspicious sideways glance. "Would this be business or social?"

Stills's laugh came deep and hearty. "You look like a filly just before she gets a bit shoved between her teeth. I regret to say that this does come under the heading of business. I want to hear more about this rustling business. I want to see what you can talk me into, and what I might be able to talk you out of, concerning it." The crinkly laugh lines at the corners of his brown eyes stood out as he smiled at Jessie. "Fair enough?"

"Fair enough," Jessie agreed earnestly. "I don't mind telling you, Hank, I need some help."

The cafe had red-and-white-checked gingham curtains hanging in the windows, and a slate blackboard listing the blue-plate specials. The deputy steered Jessie to a small table in the corner of the restaurant where they might not be seen from the street, and had a reasonable chance of not being overheard by the cafe's other patrons.

Jessie understood Stills's need to keep their time together discreet. The lawman was risking his job by associating with her in Schiff's town.

"Now," Stills began as he polished off his second slice of blueberry pie. "I've got to point out that since the Cattlemen's Association was formed, we've not been troubled by rustlers." He sipped at his coffee. "Eat your pie."

"I've got to remind you that I don't think these outlaws are real rustlers, but, as I've said, roustabouts hired by Schiff to drive the smaller spreads out of business," Jessie replied. "And I don't want my pie." She pushed the untouched wedge across the table. "You eat it."

Stills carefully stacked her plate on top of his own two empty ones. "What I won't do to please a beautiful woman."

"I don't know where you're putting it," Jessie marveled as she watched him devour the pie. Stills had hung up his hat when they'd entered the cafe. His blond curls hung past his ears. Ringlets of golden hair hung down his forehead, contrasting nicely with his skin, burnished brown by the High Plains sun.

"I burn up a lot of energy, one way or another," he replied innocently. "Why would he do it?" Stills said abruptly.

Jessie started. "You mean Schiff?"

"Back to business." Stills heaved a great, exaggerated sigh.

"He'd do it to drive Hiram Tang and his associates out of the cattle business. Using strongarm tactics like a band of phony outlaws would suit his needs perfectly. Rustlers aren't going to risk stealing cattle from big, well-manned spreads that are able to send out lynching posses, when they can steal from one-man operations like Hiram Tang's."

"I see what you're saying," Stills mused. "Nobody believes in these rustlers in the first place, but if somebody did, it would still make perfect sense that the only ranchers being stolen from are those who aren't in the Cattlemen's Association."

"Which Schiff controls," Jessie added. "Hiram told me that he tried to join, but was blackballed."

"Your daddy probably wouldn't have welcomed new competitors to Texas with open arms, either," Stills said quietly.

"Actually, he did," Jessie smiled. "But I will grant you that Texas in the seventies was a lot more in need of new blood than Wyoming is today."

"All I'm saying is that so far we've only got proof that Schiff is coldhearted toward his rivals. Now I don't approve of that," the deputy declared, "but that's probably why being pure of heart and being poor so often go together. Lots of folks would say that Tom is being a cagy businessman by taking reasonable steps against Hiram Tang and the others like him." Jessie began to speak, but Stills held up his hand to stop her. "*Reasonable* steps, is the key. Right now I'd be more suspicious of Schiff if he didn't try to increase his holdings at another's expense."

"You call rustling and gunfights reasonable means?" Jessie demanded.

"Those charges haven't yet been proved." Stills shot her a curious look. "What about motives?" he asked cannily. "Tom Schiff is mighty rich. It's understandable that he'd want to increase his acreage, but another hundred acres of grass seems like a slim reward for the risks you're saying he's taking."

Jessie wondered how far she could trust this smooth-talking, good-looking lawman. He seemed honest enough, but would he go up against the man who controlled his town? "Hank, if I tell you something, will you swear to keep it a secret?"

The deputy's boyish face took on a thoughtful, serious expression. "If I can, Miss Starbuck. If I can keep your secret, I will. But don't be revealing any kind of crime or information leading to the same, else I'll have to do my duty. Fair enough?"

"Better than that," Jessie sighed in relief. "I do believe I can trust you." She told the deputy about the coal deposits on Tang's land. She also told him about the Prussian cartel, about how her father had spent his last years battling them, and how the Prussians were responsible for the deaths of both of her parents.

Stills listened raptly to everything Jessie had to say. "These foreigners that mean to do us so much harm—why would Tom get involved with them?" The deputy looked honestly baffled. "I mean, as coldhearted as he is, Tom's still an American."

"I think I can guess at what the Prussians offered him," Jessie said. "But let's wait and see. I've already asked you to accept a great deal on faith."

"Well, this coal business sure puts a different light on things," the deputy mused. "I asked for a motive, and you sure have given me one. Schiff could triple his wealth if he got ahold of Tang's spread..."

"If I could get a message to my people in Denver, we'd

have evidence that even Forbes would have to take into account," Jessie said in agreement. "I'm sure that the agreements drawn up between Schiff and the cartel are going to be focused on mineral rights. If I had those documents, and could publicly confront him with them—"

"He'd have to lay off his strongarm tactics," Stills finished for her.

"Why, Deputy," Jessie laughed, "I do believe I've convinced you."

"It ain't funny, Miss Starbuck," Stills said quietly. "You have got me spooked. I'm starting to smell murder about to sprout, the way you can smell grass about to come up, just before spring hits the plains . . ."

"What do you think we should do?" Jessie asked. "I'm awfully worried about Hiram Tang and Ki."

Stills was silent for a moment, then he asked, *"Is* he?"

Jessie stared at him blankly.

His brown eyes searched her face. "Is this fellow named Ki what Forbes said he was?" The deputy blushed and looked down at the table. "Your boyfriend, I mean."

Now it was Jessie's turn to blush. "No. He's more like my brother."

Stills nodded quickly. "Sorry, ma'am. Guess I overstepped my bounds, asking such a personal question. Here's what I think we ought to do. Western Union will send out your wire tomorrow morning. That'll get your Denver office working on uncovering Schiff's involvement with the Prussians. You and me are going to take a little ride out to Hiram Tang's spread. We'll see how your, uh, *brother* Ki is doing. Tang will put us up for the night. That way, I can escort both him and you into town tomorrow to sign your partnership papers." He gave Jessie a sour look. "Seeing as how you had to go and practically dare Tom Schiff to stop your signing ceremony, I'd best keep an eye on you, for safety's sake."

Jessie cocked her head. "How close are you planning on sticking to me, Deputy Hank?"

He leaned back in his chair. "Well now, ma'am . . . as close as I can get."

"In that case, you'd better call me Jessie."

Grinning to beat the band, Stills put a half dollar down on the table and pushed his chair back to stand up. He grabbed his hat off the wall and said, "Jessie, let's ride."

It took them the better part of the late afternoon to ride to Tang's spread. Stills's horse, a mustard-tan cayuse, was actually smaller in size than Jessie's rented mount, a sturdy tan gelding.

"Town marshal's office owns a few of these here mongrels," the deputy said by way of explanation as they trotted along the dusty, winding trail toward the small spread. He patted his horse's neck. "These critters don't need much food and water, and they're suited for the short-range patrol work we do."

"I thought you weren't supposed to show your badge outside the town limits," Jessie teased.

"Usually we ain't needed," Stills said. "The big outfits do their own law enforcing. They've got more men to do it with than Marshal Forbes has. But like my boss said, if there's something that concerns us going on, and we want to get involved, we just mosey out and take an unofficial look around."

"Can we depend much on Forbes?" Jessie asked.

"Yep, I'll stake my life on him," Stills said firmly. "On Forbes and on the other cattlemen—I mean Schiff's friends and associates. We get proof of what you've been telling me, and the law and citizens of Nettle Grove will do what's right and just."

The shadows were lengthening. A cool breeze began to rise. It shook the branches of the cottonwood and columbine trees, turning them into sinister things that caused the horses to talk to each other in nervous whinnies.

Jessie and Stills rode around a bend in the trail and came upon Tang's home spread. It wasn't much to look at, with just a one-room cabin, a rickety-looking barn, a work shed, and a hole in the ground crisscrossed by warped wooden planks: the spread's well. An underground spring supplied Tang and his cattle with drinking water. The spring was what had made Tang pick this location in the first place, Jessie knew. Coal deposits had been the last thing on Tang's mind. A budding cattleman built his home as near to water and timber as possible, allowing his cattle to wander the range at will, knowing they'd stay near the water.

"Awfully quiet," Stills remarked thoughtfully as they rode up into Tang's front yard, scattering some scrawny hens pecking at the hard-packed earth.

"Dead quiet." Jessie shuddered as she dismounted. She let her gelding's reins trail on the ground. The horse stood still, as plains mounts were trained to do.

Jessie climbed the single step to the open front porch, knocked on the cabin's plank door, and then pushed it open. "Nobody's here," she said, turning to face Stills.

"Stay here," the deputy replied. "I'll have me a little look around." He turned his cow pony around and kneed it into a slow walk.

Jessie stood on the porch and watched him ride over to the barn. He glanced inside the open double doors, shook his head, and called over to Jessie, "No horses."

"He only had two," Jessie said to herself. And there had been a buckboard in the front yard—who took that? And where was Hiram's son?

Stills guided his mount around the cabin to where a copse of reed-thin aspens had—like Tang himself—staked out their claim near water. "Jessie!" he called. "Come around back!"

Jessie climbed down off the porch. She kept her hand on her Colt as she hurried around the side of the cabin. There had been an odd edge to Stills's normally smooth-as-honey drawl.

The deputy had dismounted. His mustard pony stood patiently behind the man, dipping its head to munch on the sparse grass. Stills's back was to Jessie. He was staring into the copse of trees, his hands on his hips.

"What's—?" Jessie began. Then she saw what he was looking at. "Oh, my God," she murmured.

It was a grave, freshly dug, and freshly filled in. A crude wooden cross stood at the grave's head. Flapping from the cross was an inscribed, bandanna-sized square of rawhide.

Stills walked to a nearby tool shed as Jessie stared at Hiram's grave. "He told me he liked these trees," she told the deputy as he returned with a shovel resting on his shoulder. "What are you going to do with that?" she asked sharply.

"You'd best go back to the house for a while, Jessie," Stills said quietly. "I've got to make sure, for the record, that—"

"That he's really buried here." Jessie nodded. "Yes, I suppose you do."

"I'll fix it just like it was, when I'm done," Stills gently promised.

Jessie took a final look at the rawhide before turning back to the cabin to wait for Stills to finish his grisly task. Carved into the leather in heartbreakingly childlike unevenness were the words:

HERE LIES HIRAM TANG

B. 1837

D. 1880

SURVIVED BY HIS LOVING SON,

DANIEL

★

Chapter 6

It was a slow, rhythmic swaying that brought Ki awake. He kept his eyes closed, not wanting to lose the last traces of his dream, for the Japanese place great stock in dreams, and Ki felt that this one had significance for him. He'd once again been a fifteen-year-old, a stowaway on that Starbuck clipper ship as it rose and fell upon the storm-tossed waves of the Pacific. In his dream he was once again concealed in the dark, clammy hold, stealthily avoiding the ship's crew, desperately longing to catch a glimpse of the sun...

Ki remembered, but kept his eyes closed, for while they were closed, he could still have hope that his sight had returned to him. Perhaps he had only dreamed that he had gone blind...

Ki opened his eyes—to shadowy darkness, blurred gray shapes against deeper black. He realized why he had wanted to remain in his dream. He had his sight in his dreams...

Ki stilled his bitter disappointment. He thought of the ancient story of the Chinese sage Chuang-tse, who dreamed he was a butterfly; when he awoke, he wondered whether he was a man who had dreamed he was a butterfly, or a butterfly dreaming he was a man.

Ki's first impulse had been to call out, "Where am I?" like some blind beggar whining for coins. No! He would not ask for help. A samurai's only purpose was to fight, and his blades could not be too dull to cut his way through this world.

Ki would fight. At once he focused his remaining senses, the way he focused his physical strength in preparation for battle.

His fingers told him that he was lying on rough wood planking, somewhat cushioned by sacks of supplies. There was the creaking of iron-rimmed wheels, the jolt and sway of travel over a rough trail; there was the clean, sharp tang of horseflesh. *I am in a wagon,* Ki realized.

Day or night? The warmth of the sun upon his skin told him that it was day, but knowing merely *that* was not good enough.

Ki lay very still, and concentrated. The warmth was strongest on his belly and chest, on his face and hands, but less intense upon the top of his head. All right, they were traveling toward the sun, but was that sun rising or setting? Was it morning or evening? Were they traveling east or west?

Ki listened. In addition to the groan and squeak of the buckboard, and the steady clopping of the horse's hooves, there was the sound of a redwing blackbird. Its song sounded more like metal scraping against metal than music, but however disharmonious its tune, Ki knew that the redwing sang in the morning.

East, then—they were traveling east, during the morning hours. Ki knew where the boy had found him: the site of the rustlers' camp. He knew what lay east of that site . . .

"Danny," he called, "why are we going toward Skinny Creek?"

"Huh?" the boy gasped. "You're awake? How'd you know where we're going? Can you see?"

"No, I'm still blind."

"Still?" the boy chuckled harshly. "You got some hope of them lights of yours coming back?"

"There is some hope of that," Ki answered gravely. During his years of apprenticeship to the master warrior Hirata, Ki had learned a great deal about medicine as well as the martial arts. His training in *atemi*—the art of striking with little force but devastating effect against a foe's pressure points—had taught him the various nerve centers of the body. Along with that knowledge came his understanding of human anatomy and physiology. A warrior had to know how to treat wounds on the battlefield. Ki knew, for example, the properties of various herbs and plants, and how they could be used either to poison or cure. In Ki's own country, training such as he had received afforded a man the same liberties and licenses as a practicing physician.

Accordingly, Ki had some idea of what had happened to him. The bullet that grazed his skull had given him a concussion. There was a swelling inside his head, and that was putting pressure on the optic nerves. "One's eyes are connected to the brain by nerves," he told the boy. "They are like wires. Think of them as telegraph wires, Danny."

"Okay," the boy said. "Your wires are down, then, right?"

Ki smiled. He sat up tentatively, ready for the pain, but it did not come. That was a good sign. It meant that the swelling might soon abate. "My lines are not exactly down. I know that because I can still see shadows. It is more like a tree has fallen across them. That tree is interfering with the telegraph messages trying to get through. Once the tree is lifted from the line, the telegraph messages should travel freely, as before."

"How does a half-breed Injun know that?" the boy demanded sarcastically.

Ki ignored the question. "Why are you going to Skinny Creek? There is no doctor there for me, and no law you can appeal to concerning your father's death. Nettle Grove, to the west—"

"Ain't looking for the law to do right by what's happened

to my pa. As for getting you to a doctor, I'm right sorry about this, but I can't get you to the doc in Nettle Grove for a while."

"Why did you not leave me back with your father's body?" Ki asked.

"First off, my pa ain't there no more. While you was sleeping I took him back to our—I mean *my* spread," the boy said harshly. "I buried him where he liked it best. As for you"—Danny's tone softened—"I reckon I should've left you, but I wasn't sure about that story of yours. You was pretty sick, and saying a lot of crazy things. Do you remember? You said you had friends coming to get you?"

"Yes," Ki said. "The story was true. They would have helped you as well, Danny."

"Well, I wasn't sure you knew what you was saying. And I couldn't leave a newly blind man all by himself." Danny paused. "I should've, but I couldn't."

"I understand," Ki said softly. "I thank you, Danny. You acted like a man of honor. You did the right thing."

"Right thing for you, maybe," the boy grumbled. "But now I'm stuck with a helpless half-breed Injun. I'm telling you right now I don't aim to travel slow for your comfort!" The boy paused. "Those friends of yours—would they follow our trail?"

"Yes," Ki said. "They will help us."

"Don't want their help," Danny said with determination. "I aim to get those murdering outlaws on my own. I'm going to make them pay for killing my father!"

Ki sat silent. He was stunned. "And you are following their trail to Skinny Creek?" he asked finally.

"That's right. They're so damned cocky they ain't tried to disguise it ! They know the Nettle Grove law ain't going to chase them. Neither will the regulators who work for Mr. Tom Schiff's Cattlemen's Association. It's up to me to kill the men who killed my pa." His voice suddenly broke. "I buried him real nice. I did it the best I could. I was tired, though, after hauling you and him up into the wagon, then hauling him down, and digging that hole...oh, damn!

Oh, damn!" he half whispered, half sobbed.

Ki heard the sound of the boy flicking his reins against the back of the horse. "Gitty-up! Gitty-up now!" the boy scolded. "What's your name, Injun?" Danny asked.

"My name is Ki." It was obvious to the samurai that the boy was fighting against his tears. The quiver in Danny's voice was a heartrending thing to hear.

"Ki, huh?" Danny tried to lighten his voice. "Like a key in a lock, right? I had a hound named Keyhole once. Named him that 'cause he had a black mark shaped like a keyhole right over one eye. He was a good old hound, but he got the distemper and he died . . ."

The boy's voice faded away to nothing. Ki sat listening to the wagon. "Danny?"

"Everything dies!" the boy wept. "Cattle, dogs, people—everything good gets killed by the bad!"

Ki listened to the low, wet sounds of the boy's grief. There was nothing he could say to comfort him, and in truth, Ki did not want to cut short the boy's mourning for his murdered father. With his father dead, the boy was all alone in the world.

Cry now, Ki thought as he listened to the sobs wracking Danny. *When your tears have dried, your childhood will have been finished. You will have to face the world, and your chosen enemies, as a man.*

Danny's crying finally tapered off. "I'm sorry," the boy murmured after a while. "I'm all through crying now."

"There is nothing dishonorable about grief," Ki encouraged. "A man can cry among his friends, but not among his enemies."

"What do you want me to do with you when it's time for me to brace those rustlers?" Danny asked, his voice now matter-of-fact, as if he were trying to make Ki forget that he'd been crying only a few moments ago.

"There is no need for you to brace them, Danny," Ki said earnestly. "The law cannot ignore your father's murder."

"I wish you was right," Danny muttered. "But you ain't

lived here the way I have. They all thought my pa was a troublemaker, just 'cause he happened to settle in Wyoming. Oh, sure, they'd pretend to round up a posse—most likely Tom Schiff would volunteer his men—and they'd pretend to look for the outlaws, but they wouldn't find them. Then Marshal Forbes would say that it was too bad, but it looked as though they'd made it out of the territory. I can't go to any other law, I'm just a kid. Who'd back my play?"

Ki flinched at the bitterness in the boy's voice. "I would. I was there. I saw some of their faces."

"But now you're blind," the boy snarled. "Fine pair of witnesses we are! A boy and a blind, half-breed Injun—"

Danny abruptly stopped talking. Ki wondered if the boy was embarrassed by his sudden outburst. "Danny, I am not an Indian," Ki began.

"That's too bad," the boy murmured uneasily. "Maybe you could have talked to *them*."

"Who is there?" Ki asked in frustration. He peered, but could see no movement through the dark fog before his eyes.

"Utes," the boy said. "I count six of them, about a mile from us, up on a ridge to our right."

"No more than six?" Ki asked.

"All I can count," the boy replied. "They're just setting on their horses and watching us. They look like a line of magpies setting on a fencerail, watching to make sure all's clear before they raid the garden."

"I have heard talk of a band of Ute renegades from the Ouray Reservation," Ki told Danny. "It was said that these Indians have killed at least one family."

"Oh, Lord!" Danny gulped. "They're riding down toward us!"

"How old are you, Danny?" Ki asked.

"What?" the boy blurted, distracted. "Oh, I'm almost fourteen!"

Ki was shocked at how young Danny was. "Between us," he smiled, "I thought you were at least seventeen. But the fact that you are so young will help us." Ki shrugged off his tattered shirt and tore a fresh strip from its hem.

Danny stared at the samurai's muscular arms and belly. "Damn, you look strong. If you only had your eyes . . . Hey! What are you doing?"

"Letting the Utes know straight off that I am blind," Ki replied. He tied the folded strip of cotton cloth across his eyes, as if it were a blindfold.

"The cut over your eye is closed pretty good," Danny observed as Ki tossed away the old dirty bandage. "It's scabbed over. Your hair covers it pretty much."

"That's good to know, but I don't think our renegade friends are that particular about their victims' appearances."

"You're pretty cool for a blind man about to get killed by Injuns," Danny sputtered. "Guess this is up to me."

"We are not dead yet," Ki said. He paused, hearing the sound of a rifle's lever being worked. "Danny! Keep your gun down, out of sight!"

"I'm just getting ready for the battle. They're almost here!" Danny's quavering voice betrayed his fear.

"Listen to me," Ki ordered as he hoisted himself up to sit on the buckboard's driving bench, beside Danny. "How many weapons do we have?"

"Just this Winchester, an ax, and a butcher's knife," the boy replied. "And twenty rounds of ammunition."

"Stop the wagon," Ki commanded. "Hide your rifle beneath your supplies."

"Then how will I get to it?" Danny asked.

"You are not going to!" Ki said impatiently. "Do as I tell you! There is not much time." The samurai felt the boy appraising him. "You must trust me if we are to survive to avenge your father's murder." He could almost hear the wheels turning in Danny's head. The boy had to cooperate if they were to survive . . .

Danny clucked the horse to a halt. "I'm hiding the rifle beneath the tent," he muttered.

"Good!" Ki evaluated how effective he could be with either the boy's ax or the knife. Neither was the weapon of choice for a sightless warrior. What he needed was a weapon light enough to whip around, and long enough to extend his reach and in that way decrease his margin of error . . .

"Danny, you mentioned a tent," Ki said. "Does it have a onepiece, center pole?"

"Yeah." There came the sound of Danny rummaging around in the bed of the wagon. "Be careful," the boy warned. "Here, I'm handing it to you. It's about five feet long."

Ki quickly ran his hands along the pole to examine it. It was about an inch and a quarter thick. Both ends of the pole were sheathed in metal. The ends were not sharp, but rounded, as the pole was not meant to be driven into the ground. Ki held the pole in one hand and twirled it above his head like a baton. The pole was unbalanced, but that was to be expected; it was, after all, merely a tent post. All things considered, it would serve admirably.

"What are you gonna do with that stick?" Danny asked, fascinated. "You sure can handle it!"

"There is no finer weapon for a blind man than a *bo* staff," Ki replied. "Danny, hand me the kitchen knife." It was an ungainly, wooden-handled, rather dull blade, barely suitable for chopping onions. Still, its point was serviceable, and a knife might come in handy. Ki placed it beneath the bench seat of the buckboard. "Are the Utes close enough for you to make out their weapons?"

"Only one rifle," Danny answered. "The other five got bows." He sat back down beside Ki, and took up the reins.

"Good!" Ki sighed in relief. "The one with the rifle will consider it beneath his dignity to use a firearm on the likes of us. They will fire arrows at us, not bullets."

"I don't see why being turned into pincushions is so comforting a notion to you," Danny growled. When Ki laughed, the boy added quietly, "Glad you're here. Didn't want to die alone. With you here, I ain't so scared."

"Are you smiling, Danny?" Ki asked gently.

"Yeah," the boy admitted shyly.

"Excellent!" Ki declared. "Nothing is more unnerving

to an adversary than to be confronted with a smile."

"They're here!" Danny hissed.

"No quick moves," Ki warned. More to give the boy something to do than anything else, he said, "Describe them for me." Meanwhile he listened to the sound of the approaching Utes' horses. Their hooves clamored like thunder.

"All six are young looking," Danny said hurriedly. "Not one looks more than twenty."

That is to our disadvantage, Ki thought. *But it is as expected*. Older, more mature Ute braves would have more respect for his blindness; but then, older braves never went renegade. It was the young men, bored with reservation life and itching to make a name for themselves as warriors, who jumped the reservation. Renegade bands rarely numbered more than a handful of close friends and cousins. The young braves would amuse themselves, whooping and hollering, until an army patrol came around to escort them back to the reservation. They were not punished unless they had committed some crime while they were on their brief adventure.

The thudding of hooves quieted. Ki could smell a sweet, coppery scent as he listened to the Utes murmuring among themselves.

"Oh, Lord," Danny muttered. "They're carrying scalps!"

These renegades would be desperate men, Ki realized. The army would either shoot them on sight or take them back to be hanged for murder.

"We see you are a boy and a blind man," one of the Utes called out. "We will spare your lives. Give us your belongings and we shall—"

"No," Ki intoned, cutting the Ute off in mid-sentence. He was grateful that at least one of them could speak English. "If you leave us now, in peace, I shall spare *your* lives." He heard the buckboard's bench creak as Danny stiffened with horror beside him. "Say nothing!" Ki hissed to the boy out of the side of his mouth. "I do all the talking!"

"A blind man cannot hurt us!" the Ute brave laughed.

Ki said nothing, but only smiled toward where the brave's voice was coming from. This was the first battle in their war of nerves, and Ki intended to win it. To occupy himself, he pictured in his mind's eye the general physical characteristics of the Utes he had seen. They tended to have large round heads, with moon faces. They were a short-statured people with short arms and bandy legs, but their torsos were strong. Utes were built like bears, and were just as doggedly fierce when challenged. As a tribe they were peaceful and friendly, but all renegades were dangerous, be they white, red, or yellow.

At last the Ute spokesman conceded the first battle. "How could a blind man hurt us?" he sulked. "You need strong medicine *now,* blind man! Maybe you should show more respect!"

Ki used the tentpole to measure the distance from the buckboard's seat to the ground, and once that was established in his mind, he hopped gracefully down. He used the pole as a blind man's cane, waving it before him just inches above the ground as he strode to a spot between the Utes and the buckboard. Now he grasped the pole in its center, holding it horizontally across his chest.

"I have strong medicine," he called to the Utes. "It is you who should show respect. A great, fierce spirit lives inside of me."

"I think you're a liar, blind man," the Ute spat. "I think I will search your wagon now." He clucked his pony into a walk toward Ki. The Ute meant to win the second battle of nerves.

The samurai held the pole vertically and began to spin it in front of himself in a figure-eight pattern. He rotated his hips and shoulders in order to give the pole more speed. Soon it was a buzzing, whooshing blur.

Any horse will start at a nearby, sudden movement. The Ute's pony was no exception. Confronted by the man-sized windmill that Ki had become, the pony reared up on its hind legs. The Indian lost his composure as he fought to regain control of his mount.

Ki heard it all: the nervous whinnying of the pony, its bucking and snorting, and the low-pitched oaths of its Indian rider. During the confusion he heard Danny's whispered warning: "The one you're up against right now has the rifle."

And I have my staff, Ki thought contentedly. *My staff shall be my eyes, fists, and feet.*

The Ute had calmed his pony. Once again the renegade Indian kneed his mount into a forward walk. Ki waited and listened, his staff at rest across his shoulder. The pony's plodding steps grew closer. "Get out of my way!" the Ute snarled.

Ki rocked back and forth on his bare feet. His toes gripped the ground, took root.

"Watch out!" Danny cried in alarm.

Ki heard the boy only faintly. All of his attention was focused on the approaching Ute. He was a warrior, and did not need his eyes. All he needed was an enemy to fight.

Ki waited until the last possible second. He waited until he could feel the horse's wet breath on his face, and the mount's body heat radiating. He waited until droplets of the horse's sweat stung him, and its smell filled his nose.

And then the samurai leaped lightly aside. He lifted the tentpole from his shoulder and whipped it about in a roundhouse swing that just tickled the horse's ears, but caught the Ute across his moon face. The Indian's pony bucked in terror while the stunned Ute fell backward.

Ki listened to the satisfying grunt as the Ute thudded to the ground, his rifle's stock shattering against a rock. That firearm would kill no more families, the samurai grinned to himself.

The fallen Ute was literally growling in fury. Ki homed in on the sound. He reversed his grip on the tentpole to hold it as if it were a broom. He swept one metal-tipped end along the ground, digging a furrow, and then using a powerful flick of his wrists to scoop up some dust and dirt and fling it into the Ute's face.

The Ute's cry of pain as he rubbed at his dirt-filled eyes told Ki that he had been on target. "Now we are both blind," he announced to the moaning Indian, at the same time bringing around the tentpole to slam it against the side of the Ute's head. Ki heard the man hit the ground, and then he heard nothing else from the Ute. Evidently he was lying quite still.

The samurai backed up, feeling his way with his pole and his hands, until he'd reached the side of the buckboard. "What are they doing now, Danny?" he murmured.

"That was—" the boy began. "I mean—I—I—"

"Thank you, Danny," Ki smiled. "But quickly! What are the rest of them doing now?"

"Nothing," the boy said, his voice the equivalent of a shrug. "They're just looking at us, and the one you've knocked out, and talking."

"Yes. I wish one of us understood their language." Ki reached up and felt around until he found Danny's hand, and gave it a reassuring squeeze. "Do not fear. The one gun they had is now broken, is it not?"

"Yep!" Danny said. "How'd you know when to do that with the tentpole? Just what kind of Injun are you?"

"A kind these Utes have never before met!" Ki chuckled. The thrill of combat had given him back his high spirits. He considered removing his blindfold, so as to at least see the shadowy shapes of his enemies, but decided against that. A samurai did not do things by halves. No sight at all was a more honorable alternative than the pitiful half-sight of an old man. Besides, the world of shadows and fog would distract Ki from fully utilizing his other senses.

"Oh, Lord!" Danny breathed. "One of them is hocking an arrow!"

Ki quickly danced away from the buckboard. He did not want the boy to be in the line of fire. "Danny! Is he aiming at me?" Ki demanded.

"Yes," Danny whimpered. "You can't—"

"Quiet!" Ki ordered. No verbal exchange was needed between himself and the man drawing a bead upon him. Ki had often felt the eternal link between the archer and the target—the only unusual thing this time was that he was the target!

Time itself seemed to slow as Ki stood quietly. He held his makeshift staff diagonally across his torso. He regulated his breathing, channeling all of his awareness into his remaining four physical senses, and into a *sixth* sense known as *haragei*—the warrior's sense of survival.

A samurai needed only the will to go on fighting, and *haragei* was both the origin and product of that will. There was nothing mystical about it. If one was the right sort of person, one often *knew* when one was being watched, for example, or *felt* another's eyes on the back of one's neck. The samurai took those natural abilities and talents and honed them as sharply as his weapons.

Ki focused on the sound of the Ute's bowstring being drawn back. He heard, as if he were merely inches away, the squeak of the bow itself as it flexed. There was a faraway, velvety rubbing sound. It was, Ki knew, the sound produced by the light friction of the arrow's shaft as it was scraped back against the bow. All the while, he was listening to the Ute's breathing. Now that breathing stopped. The Indian was holding his breath in order to fire.

To Ki, the dull snap of the bowstring being released seemed to echo in distant canyons. The whiz of the shaft cutting through the air grew ever louder, *but time had slowed*. To Ki, the approaching sound grew steadily, but gradually. It was like the rumble of a far distant train when one presses one's ear against the rails.

At the proper moment he did not step aside, but merely leaned away from the passing arrow. In his ears, it did sound as long as a freight train as it sailed by.

Another arrow was fired. Its humming as it streaked through the air was as exquisitely perfect as the single bold black stroke of ink a Japanese artist might brush across a pristine square of rice parchment.

An artist can create beauty by stroking ink upon paper. But then there is the artist who uses the physical world as his parchment, his body as his brush, and his movements as his ink—

As the arrow sped past, Ki turned with it, as if his blind

eyes could see. He snapped out his arm, keeping his spread fingers pointing skyward, as if he were executing a *teisho-uke*, or palm-heel strike, to snatch the speeding shaft out of the air as if it were merely a fly.

"Holy shit!" Danny gasped.

The Utes began to chitter fearfully among themselves. "Let us collect our fallen brave, and go in peace," one of them pleaded with Ki. "You do have great medicine, blind man. Please spare us!"

"Go, then," Ki told them, dropping the captured arrow to the ground. He used the pole to help him find his way back to the buckboard, and boosted himself up beside Danny. "Tell me what is happening," he murmured to the awestruck boy. "I do not trust them."

"They're getting the one you knocked down, and putting him belly-down across his pony," Danny explained. "They're leaving!" he added gleefully. "How did you do all that?"

"It would take a while to explain," Ki said softly. He pulled off his blindfold. The gray, smeared light stabbed painfully into his crippled eyes, but that discomfort was nothing compared to the sharp pang of disappointment that pierced his heart. Now that the battle was over, Ki was once again left with nothing to distract him from the reality of his blindness.

"Indians, even renegades, are too proud to attack a disabled man like myself all at once," Ki continued. "I knew that I would only have to deal with them one at a time." He felt a shift in the boy's attention. "What is it, Danny?"

"Riders!" the boy said excitedly. "A whole bunch of riders coming from out of the east. Boy! Those Utes are riding for it, but they're being cut off by the— Hey!" Danny gripped Ki's arm. "Maybe these folks are your friends!"

"Perhaps," Ki said. "Can you see if there is a woman among them?"

"Nah, they're still too far away. They've caught those renegades—"

Ki heard the rattle of distant gunfire. "Danny, what's going on? The Utes had no firearms."

"I know," the boy cut him off softly. "Those riders just

shot the Utes down. Just cut them down in cold blood."

"Those are not my friends," Ki muttered. "Neither they nor the Nettle Grove town marshal would take it upon themselves to execute the Utes, no matter what their crimes. You said they were riding from the east—they could be coming from Skinny Creek. How many are there?"

"Seven," Danny replied anxiously. "Seven riders coming from Skinny Creek. That's where the rustlers' trail was leading."

"Unhitch the horse and ride away, Danny," Ki ordered.

"I ain't leaving you," the boy argued.

"Danny—"

"No!" he said flatly. "Just put that out of your head. I saved your life before, and you just saved mine. Yesterday I lost my pa," he added in a voice now grown husky. "I don't aim to lose my only friend today!"

"I see," Ki replied. "No, friends such as ourselves cannot separate," he said gently. "Forgive me for suggesting it."

"I wish you *did* see," Danny sighed wistfully. "With my rifle you could probably pick them off. They're riding toward us now. I ain't a good enough shot to try it," the boy apologized. "Not *yet,* that is," he added hotly.

"Is there any cover around?" Ki asked.

"None worth a damn," the boy replied. "And they're too close for us to make a run for it, especially since all we've got is this dumb one-horse buckboard."

Ki stared into the gray fog, waiting for the rustlers' shadowy shapes to loom into blurred view. His toes found the wooden handle of the kitchen knife lying beneath the bench seat of the wagon.

"Look what we got here!" one of the cattle thieves laughed as the band of riders trotted up to the buckboard.

"I know that kid," another man said. "That's Tang's brat."

"And this here's that chink we thought was dead," the first man said.

"You don't need your guns out," Danny announced. "Your bullets blinded him."

"That right, kid?" the first man asked with mild interest.

"What should we do, Tim?" one of the other rustlers asked. "Shoot 'em now?"

"No," Tim said. "The old man will want 'em both alive, as bargaining chips. We can always shoot 'em later. Just a kid and a blind chink . . . Listen to me, boy," he addressed Danny. "I'm the one who shot that chink's eyes out, and I'll do the same to you if you try anything."

Ki concentrated on separating the one called Tim from the indistinguishable mass that was the rustlers grouped together. *So this is the man who cost me my sight . . . if only this Tim would keep talking,* Ki thought, as his toes slid the kitchen knife into a handier position.

"Old man thinks the chink's dead already," one of the men observed.

"Don't matter," Tim said. "Him captured and a prisoner is just as good as his being dead. Besides, when I handed over his knives and bow and stuff, the old man remarked as to how he wished we'd taken him alive, so that we'd have some leverage with that Starbuck woman."

Ki had locked his awareness on to Tim's position. He'd wiggled his toes beneath the knife's blade. A flick of his foot would catapult the knife up into his hand. If he could kill their leader and push Danny out of the line of fire, and then if Ki himself could get to the Winchester buried beneath the folded tent . . .

A lot of ifs, Ki thought to himself. But any chance was worth taking to keep Danny and himself from becoming the rustlers' prisoners. Once they were hidden away, Jessie would have no chance of finding them. They would become the bait that might lure her into a trap set by her enemies. No, the samurai decided sadly. His oath to Jessie's father required that he do his utmost not even *indirectly* to jeopardize her safety. He could not become a hostage.

As for Danny—well, the boy had insisted on hunting the rustlers. Now he would have to take his chances. Ki would protect the boy with his own life, but Danny was here by choice, and would have to live out the *karma* that earlier choice now dictated.

Ki was about to make his move when Tim called out, "Let's ride."

The one large blur broke up into several smaller ones. Ki had lost Tim's position.

"Get ready to jump beneath the wagon," Ki whispered to Danny. In a louder voice he called out, "Tim?"

"Yeah?" came a voice from out of the gray fog.

Instantly, Ki zeroed in on it. The knife appeared in his hand as if by magic. He flung it at his target. Hope rose inside the samurai as he heard the blade hit home, and heard the rustler's startled cry. But even as Ki was shoving Danny to the ground, strong fingers wound themselves into his thick black hair. He was jerked out of the buckboard to land roughly upon the ground. He climbed to his feet, only to be spun around and around by the horsemen crowding him with their mounts. The dizziness caused Ki to lose his bearings. He no longer knew where the buckboard was. A horse slammed into him, and once more he went sprawling. The metallic sounds of weapons being cocked, and a rough voice saying, "Don't move!" convinced the samurai that on the ground was the best place to remain.

"Danny?" Ki called out. "Are you all right? What happened?"

"Get the kid back into the wagon," Tim growled. "As for you, chink, I'm going to pay you back for this. When it's time for you to die, I'm going to be the one to do the killing! Throw him in the back of the wagon!" he ordered his men. "Let's go!"

Ki was hauled to his feet and unceremoniously tossed into the bed of the buckboard. Danny cradled Ki's head in his lap as the buckboard began to creak and sway. One of the rustlers was doing the driving.

"Damn, that cut above your eye has opened up again," Danny mumbled.

"Are you all right?" Ki repeated faintly. He himself was feeling quite weak from being knocked about. He had yet to fully regain his physical strength since his concussion, and the awesome concentration that had been required to defeat the Utes had further whittled away his small reserve of vitality. "They did not hurt you?"

"I'm fine," Danny promised him. "That was a crazy thing for you to do," the boy whispered. "And what's even crazier is that it almost worked."

"What *did* happen?" Ki begged. "I heard the knife hit him. I heard his cry."

"You *did* hit him," the boy said sadly. "But that kitchen knife ain't got proper balance for throwing. The blade turned itself around so that the knife hit him handle first. You sure scared the hell out of him, though." He tried to laugh, but the sound died in his throat as he glanced at the hard, professional gunmen who had taken them captive.

"We will get out of this, Danny," Ki mumbled against the pain inside his head. "Now I must rest . . . must sleep." The throbbing had returned with a vengeance.

"You do that," Danny comforted. "You sleep now." He stared at the strange man who had fought by his father's side at the cost of his eyes, the man who had just now twice risked his life to protect a boy he hardly knew, the man who now looked so drawn, so pale. Danny began to fear for his life. He brought Ki's fingers up to his face.

"Feel it?" the samurai heard the boy say just before he drifted off. "Can you tell?" Danny whispered. "I'm smiling at these bastards. I'm smiling at our enemies, like you'd do . . ."

★

Chapter 7

Sam Dunn was the only attorney in Nettle Grove who had been willing to draw up the legal papers that would finalize the partnership between Hiram Tang and Jessica Starbuck. All the other lawyers—and Nettle Grove had a baker's dozen—refused to have anything to do with the deal because they were all afraid of offending Tom Schiff.

Dunn had taken on the case because he firmly believed that the future would bring changes in Wyoming Territory, and in the power elite that controlled the township. He was able to believe this because he was a young man, and poor. He had no vested interest in keeping things from changing.

Dunn's office was just a front-parlor room in a second-class boarding house located in a back alley off Main Street. His one room was crowded with mismatched office furniture, a narrow cot which was where he slept at night, and tall, rickety bookshelves crammed with the secondhand law volumes that had been his entire world for his last three years in school.

But even a newly minted lawyer like Dunn was able to

see that Jessica Starbuck was about to make Hiram Tang and the other ranchers Dunn was representing rich men. That was why, despite his fervent desire to impress the extremely rich, rather famous, and strikingly lovely Jessica Starbuck, he could not keep from showing his shock and disappointment at Jessie's news of Tang's death.

Jessie and Deputy Hank Stills had spent an uneasy night at Tang's ranch. Stills had dug up the body to verify that Hiram Tang was really dead, and then had reburied the rancher's corpse. At dawn, he and Jessie had ridden back to Nettle Grove. Stills had gone to fetch Marshal Forbes, while Jessie had gone directly to Dunn's office.

Now the four of them—Jessie, Forbes, Stills, and Dunn—sat in the lawyer's office, as the deputy told the marshal what he'd found.

"Hiram Tang had been shot twice, in the back," the deputy explained, running his fingers through his blond curls. "His son, Danny, had buried him. There was no sign of the kid around the spread."

"You think he's run off?" Forbes asked.

"I was at the spread the day before," Jessie cut in. "They had two horses and a buckboard. One horse was shot yesterday morning, *by the rustlers,*" she emphasized, giving Forbes a dirty look.

"Well, there was no wagon or horse at the spread while we were there," Hank continued. "Some supplies were missing as well. I reckon the kid lit out after the cow thieves who did in his papa."

"Not you too?" Forbes scowled at his deputy. "There's *still* no evidence to support Miss Starbuck's rustler story."

"Then who shot Hiram?" Jessie demanded.

Forbes shrugged. "That's something we still have to find out," the potbellied, balding marshal grimaced. "For one thing, we know that there's a bunch of Ute renegades in the area. Maybe they did the killing. Like an Injun to shoot a man in the back..."

"Not how it happened, Marshal," Stills said. His big brown eyes reminded Jessie of a doleful hound's as the deputy glanced apologetically at Attorney Dunn. "I don't rightly know if what I did was legal, but since I'd already gone to the trouble of digging Hiram up, I thought I might as well find out as much as I could about the shooter who put the poor fellow in the ground." The deputy pulled a couple of bits of lead out of the breast pocket of his gray flannel shirt. "These are the slugs I found in Hiram. They're .41-caliber revolver rounds."

"Damn," Forbes muttered. "Those Utes might have an odd rifle or shotgun, but unless the Bureau of Indian Affairs has taken to supplying them with handguns, those pistol slugs clear the renegades." He offered Jessie a sheepish smile. "Don't suppose you found one of those running irons lying around?"

"No I didn't," Jessie sighed. "I also didn't find my friend Ki. Marshal Forbes, I'm very worried about him."

"Maybe he's with Danny," Deputy Stills offered. "At least we didn't find a body, Jessie. From what you've told me about Ki, that fellow can take care of himself."

"Excuse me," Dunn interrupted. He took off his wire-rimmed spectacles and polished them against the rather bedraggled points of his gray satin vest. "I do sympathize with your concern—um, uh, *concerning* your friend—" He blushed. "But our, uh, real concern—"

"If *concerns* were bullets, son, you'd be about out of ammo," Forbes remarked mildly. "Quit trying to impress the lady and come out with what you're trying to say."

Dunn stared down at the neat pile of documents he had yesterday prepared for the signatures of Jessica Starbuck and Hiram Tang. "What I'm trying to say is that if this partnership is not to fall apart, Mr. Tang's son must be found, and the boy must be alive and well if he's to sign these." He tapped the pile of agreements.

"But Danny is only fourteen!" Jessie argued. "How can a minor sign his name to such an important negotiation?"

"Well, he is young," Dunn agreed, "but this is Wyoming Territory, Miss Starbuck. A lot of very important men started themselves on the road to their fortunes when they were Danny's age. As it now stands, Danny will inherit the spread. He can no longer represent the other ranchers the way his father was going to, but they can all sign for themselves. That's only a minor revision of the contracts."

"Why can't the other ranchers just pick themselves another representative to take Hiram's place?" Forbes asked. "That seems to me to be the easiest thing to do."

Deputy Stills looked questioningly at Jessie. "I guess we'd better fill the marshal in," he suggested. "About the coal?"

"I guess you'd better!" Forbes said gruffly. "Just what's going on?"

Jessie hesitated, but Stills said, "Trust me," and she had to admit to herself that she did trust this handsome, honest deputy. Last night she'd expected Stills to make a sexual advance toward her, but it hadn't happened. The deputy had come back to the cabin after his grisly investigation of Tang's corpse had been completed. Stills had removed his vest and shirt while he'd been digging up and then refilling the grave. His well-muscled torso and arms had glistened with sweat in the light of the hearth fire Jessie had built to cook them a ham-and-eggs supper assembled from the spread's modest larder.

She'd waited for Stills to try and sweep her up into his arms, as they'd sipped at their coffee. In truth, she'd wanted him to, and the intense look in his brown eyes told her that the same thoughts were running through his head.

But nothing had happened. The deputy had finished his coffee, gathered up a couple of blankets, drapped his holstered .44 across his broad shoulder, and excused himself for the night, saying that he enjoyed sleeping under the stars, and that she could have the cabin all to herself. His sweet, bashful manner, combined with her anguish over Ki's whereabouts and well-being, had reduced her to tears. When she awoke the next morning, she found that he'd saddled both of their horses for the ride back to Nettle Grove.

As they mounted up, Stills had leaned across his own saddle to briefly take her hand and murmur shyly, "I've got to tell you that next to this morning's sunrise, you're the prettiest thing I could ever hope to see."

Now, in response to Stills's prodding, Jessie told Marshal Forbes what she'd learned concerning the coal deposits on Tang's land. "So you see, Marshal," she finished, "the other ranchers could pick themselves a new representative, but it's the Tang spread that Tom Schiff really wants, and not for grazing purposes."

Forbes nodded. He tugged thoughtfully at the shoulder harness holding his hogleg .45 in place. "I said before that your were a fine actress, miss. And now I'm becoming a fine audience. Why in tarnation didn't you tell me about these here coal deposits before?" Forbes shook his shiny bald head. "The only thing that was keeping me from believing you was that I couldn't for the life of me figure out why a rich man like Tom Schiff would break the law just to get himself a few more acres of grazing land. But a fortune in coal—!"

"I guess I should have told you, Marshal," Jessie admitted. "But, truth to tell, I didn't exactly trust you . . ." she trailed off.

"Well, can't say that I gave you much cause to trust me," Forbes muttered. "But I hope Hank here has convinced you that I'm on the up-and-up. Tom Schiff's got a lot of influence in Nettle Grove, but we citizens—and that includes his fellow cattlemen in the association—want our township to be a place of pride. I *still* think Tom has a rightful claim to the land, but he'd better exercise that claim in a just and law-abiding manner, or I'll throw his ass—oops! Excuse me, miss!" Forbes stammered in embarrassment. "I meant—"

"I understand what you meant," Jessie smiled. "And I'm thankful to have your help."

"Back to business," Dunn said briskly. "We now understand why Danny must be found alive and well. If he is, the whole town will stand behind his holding on to his father's spread. Any number of honest citizens would help him make a go of his ranch."

"That's true," Forbes nodded. "But if the boy isn't found, Tom Schiff has the clout to sway his fellow cattlemen over to his point of view. Schiff trying to cheat a boy of his rightful inheritance is one thing, but Schiff merely laying claim to land nobody else has a hold on is quite another."

"Marshal Forbes, will you put together a posse to help me search for Danny and my friend Ki?" Jessie asked.

Forbes looked uneasy as he pondered her request. "I sure do wish we had a little more solid evidence before I went against Tom."

Jessie began to get angry, but Stills calmed her down, saying, "Look at it from the marshal's point of view. All Schiff would have to do is call a cattlemen's meeting to get Forbes fired."

The marshal nodded. "I need something on Tom to fight back with if that should happen. Be reasonable, Miss Starbuck! I can't be of much use to you if I'm out of a job, now can I?"

"I guess you're right, Marshal," Jessie said slowly. "Oh, how I wish Ki were here. I feel so alone." She felt her eyes grow wet with tears of concern for her friend.

"Hey, come on now," Stills soothed in his honeyed drawl. "You ain't alone."

"Damn right!" Forbes nodded adamantly. His own voice sounded a mite husky. "We'll find your friend, and we'll take good care of you, won't we, Hank?"

"For sure," Hank grinned. "Say, your wire should have been sent this morning." The deputy dug out his battered pocket watch and checked the time. "It's after two. Maybe some kind of answer has come back."

"Answer concerning what?" Forbes asked sharply.

Stills laughed. "Fill you in on the way to the telegraph office, boss."

"Don't see why I always got to be the last to know," Forbes groused. "You there, son," the marshal commanded

Dunn as they made ready to leave his office. "Keep them papers ready. I aim to see that Tang's boy gets what's coming to him!"

"Yes, sir!" Dunn smiled. He tried not to stare too closely as Jessie wiggled her round, denim-sheathed backside through the obstacle course of his furniture. Maybe he would get to collect his fees on this deal, after all. The young lawyer certainly hoped so. He'd already used the retainer Jessie had paid him to cover three months' worth of back rent.

Jessie filled the marshal in on her suspicions concerning Schiff and the Prussian cartel as the three of them headed for the telegraph office. Forbes couldn't understand what might make an American sell out his own country.

"That's because you may be ugly, stubborn, and fat," Hank joshed, "but you ain't greedy, boss. I've been pondering what Jessie's told us, and it's occurred to me that the railroad may not want that coal for years. Old Tom can't wait that long, but I'll wager a month's pay that years are nothing to these Prussians."

"That's right," Jessie frowned. "Let's suppose that the cartel has already paid Schiff hard cash for what the Prussians will profit by in years to come?"

"I get it," Forbes said sourly. "Tom has sold what he don't yet rightly own. What a sweet setup! He's got his cash, he's got no-goods pretending to be rustlers in order to run Tang and his friends into the red, and then Schiff gets to refuse to loan them fresh capital they'd need to hold on to their spreads. Yep," the marshal grinned. "Tom had it all tied up neater than a calf at branding time—but then *you* arrived, Miss Starbuck!"

"He may still have us hogtied," Jessie muttered. "Do you believe in feminine intuition, Marshal?"

"I do, when the female who's getting the hunch is as feminine as you, little miss!" Forbes sniggered, nudging a blushing Deputy Stills in the ribs.

"What's on your mind, Jessie?" Stills groaned.

"Ki had trailed the rustlers to Skinny Creek, where, according to him, their trail simply disappeared," Jessie explained. "If it were up to me, that's where I'd start my search for Ki and Danny."

"You think they're together?" Stills asked.

Jessie shrugged. "I think that Ki went after the rustlers."

"If he wasn't wounded, or worse," Stills said softly. "Look, Jessie. I want your friend to be safe and sound for your sake, but you've got to face facts. Trailing a band of cow thieves is dangerous work."

"It's just that if Ki were dead, I think I'd *feel* it, somehow," Jessie fretted. She shook herself briskly, tossing back her golden tresses. "If Ki was on his way to Skinny Creek, and came across Danny, he'd have taken the boy along. Assuming that they're both alive, I'll wager that they're together."

Forbes led the way into the shacklike Western Union office. The same pink-cheeked young clerk was on duty, but today he looked drawn and worried.

"This lady's wire go out this morning, Jeff?" Forbes asked.

The clerk shook his head. "Line's down, Marshal."

"What!"

"Been down since I opened up this morning," the clerk continued. He turned to Jessie. "I showed up bright and early to send your wire, ma'am. That's how I found out we was cut off."

"Well, how long, boy?" Forbes snorted. "When's this damn thing gonna get fixed?"

The clerk colored. "Can't rightly say, sir. There's a lot of miles of wire between us and the next railway depot, in Cough Creek. Western Union's supposed to have riders out daily checking the wire, but . . ."

"What's your feminine intuition say about this, Jessie?" Stills asked grimly.

"All right, all right, simmer down," Forbes calmed his deputy. "We ain't licked yet." He tilted his head toward the clerk, who was all ears. "Let's discuss this outside," he murmured to Jessie and Stills.

"I'll send this wire as soon as I can," the clerk piped cheerfully as they clomped out of the office.

"Well, that takes care of our getting any evidence on Schiff and the Prussians," Jessie said dismally, once they were out of the clerk's hearing.

"Don't be too sure," Forbes growled. "Hank, ain't it strange that the telegraph wire should cross a corner of Tom Schiff's land?"

"Just what I was thinking, boss," the deputy drawled. "But, hell," he muttered irritably, "life's just filled with coincidences." He glanced at Jessie. "That's a joke, ma'am."

"I wish I felt like laughing..."

"We may get the last laugh, after all," Forbes said. He tipped his hat to Jessie. "Pardon my language, but old Tom is starting to piss me off!"

Laughing, Jessie implusively threw her arms around the marshal to plant a kiss smack on his bald head. "I'm so sorry I misjudged you," she sweetly apologized.

"Shucks," Forbes said, but he was glowing as red as an overloaded woodstove.

"What's our next move, boss?" Stills chuckled.

"Time for you and me to try out for the theater," Forbes winked. "I don't want Tom to realize that I've come around to Miss Starbuck's way of thinking," he explained. "When we get back to the office, I suspect that Schiff will be waiting there to find out what's going on."

"And you'll have to tell him?" Jessie asked.

"Got to," Forbes nodded. "Else he'll suspect something's up. I want him to consider me nice and tame until I get the evidence to back your charges against him. If and when I get that evidence, I'll put the cuffs on him, and I'll be able to do it without fear of losing my badge." He shrugged. "Until then, it's still Tom Schiff's town."

"And we can't challenge him and hope to win," Stills added.

"Right," Forbes said wryly. "Now, Tom's going to want to organize a search party or two to find the boy—"

“It doesn’t take much imagination to know what’ll happen to Danny if Schiff finds him.” Jessie warned.

“I suspect Tom will want to steer us clear of Skinny Creek,” Forbes agreed. The marshal’s pudgy face took on a crafty look. He put his arm around Stills and led him away from Jessie, calling, “Let me set up this bit of playacting without you, Miss Starbuck. It’ll go over a lot better if you’re as surprised as everyone else is gonna be!”

★

Chapter 8

A shout to "Hurry it up!" from one of the rustlers snapped Ki awake. He had been dreaming of Jessie, protecting her from some menace . . . But the rustler's voice and the jolting progress of the buckboard brought the samurai back to the present, and reminded him that—if anything—now he needed Jessie's protection.

"How are you?" Danny asked quietly.

Ki sat up, very tentatively. "The pain is gone," he smiled. The throbbing had indeed disappeared, and the samurai thought that he could detect some slight improvement in his vision. The world was still a blur, but Ki's ability to detect light had increased to the extent where he had to avert his gaze from the brilliance of the sun, which now appeared to him as a fiery stain upon the gray fog.

As excited as he was, Ki did not tell Danny about the improvement. For one thing, he did not want to build up the boy's—and his own—hopes too much. It could well turn out that it was not his blindness that was temporary, but the improvement . . .

For another thing, he did not dare let the rustlers know

that he might be getting better. They were willing to let a blind man live, but there was no saying what they might do to him if they thought he was regaining his sight.

"Where are we?" Ki asked the boy. "What time is it?" It seemed to him as if the sun were setting, but he could not be sure.

"Late afternoon," Danny replied. "The sun is setting behind us. We're heading east."

"To Skinny Creek?"

"Seems that way."

"Hold it up!" the rustler named Tim suddenly ordered his men.

"What's wrong?" Ki whispered as they slowed to a halt.

"Lie easy," Danny said fretfully. "He's noticed that you're awake. Now he's coming over."

The boy watched the outlaw leader wheel his horse around to draw up beside the buckboard. The man pulled his Colt and leaned from the saddle to press the cocked gun against Ki's head.

"Two of you men fetch some rope to tie this chink up," Tim snarled. "Don't worry, I got him covered."

"But he's blind," one of the cow thieves protested.

"Blind or not, tie him up!" Tim repeated. "You all seen what he did with that knife. Are you forgetting how he killed two of us back when he was sided with this brat's father?"

Two of the rustlers hurried to pull Ki's arms forward and lash them together.

"Don't forget his legs," Tim warned, his pistol still on Ki. "You seen how he can kick. Don't hogtie him, but give him some slack, like you was hobbling a horse," he instructed. "That way he'll be able to shuffle along and care for himself, but he won't be able to do anything to us."

When it was done, Tim holstered his gun and took up his position at the front of the party. "Let's go. Skinny Creek's just over the next rise."

"Are those ropes too tight?" Danny worried.

No, Ki mouthed silently. Then he said out loud, "I cannot

feel my hands and feet, they are so tight!"

"Better that than a bullet," the rustler who was driving the buckboard said complacently, glancing over his shoulder. "Least you're alive, Chinaman." Then he turned his attention back to the trail.

Danny patted Ki on the shoulder to let him know that he had understood the ruse. Ki wished that he could further comfort the boy, but his fear of being overheard kept him from doing so.

The fact was, as soon as the outlaws had begun to twist the rope around his limbs, the samurai had expanded his powerful wrist and ankle muscles. Now that his muscles were relaxed, he had some slack to play with in both knotted coils. It would take him a while—and cost him some skin—but he could eventually wiggle free, when the time was right.

"It looks like we're done for," Danny moped. "We're dead for sure."

"Why do you say that?" Ki scolded. "There is no reason for them to kill you."

"Don't lie to me. I've seen their faces and they've out-and-out admitted to killing my father. Their hideout's in Skinny Creek, and hell! They're taking us there." Danny's laugh was grim, and sounded like that of a man twice his fourteen years. "Ain't no way we're getting out of this."

"So far, they have gone to some trouble not to kill us," Ki pointed out. "Until they speak to their boss, this 'old man' they keep referring to—"

"That'd be Tom Schiff."

"You are a very clever young man," Ki chuckled. "Yes, I believe they *do* work for Schiff, but my point is that they will not harm us until they confer with him. They cannot do that before morning, and then they must return to Skinny Creek. That gives us another day." Here Ki lowered his voice to the barest whisper. "Another day to plot our escape, and another day for my friend to bring help."

"You mean Miss Starbuck. I met her, don't forget!" Danny sighed. "I don't know what kind of help she can expect in Nettle Grove. My pa wasn't too popular with the marshal and all."

"You are indeed clever," Ki said, troubled. "She will do all she can for us."

"And you yourself told me that you tracked these men to Skinny Creek, and then lost them. If you couldn't find their hideout, how's a *girl* gonna do it?"

"Girls can be very helpful," Ki said. " *And* resourceful. "When you are older, you will learn to appreciate them."

Danny's faint chuckle told Ki that he had succeeded in raising the frightened boy's low spirits. To himself, the samurai had to admit that Danny's dismal assessment of their predicament was much more realistic than his own optimism. There were seven rustlers. Blind as he was, Ki had little chance of defeating them, even if he did get himself out of his ropes. Jessie was more than likely having trouble getting help, and even if she did manage to persuade a posse to accompany her, the whereabouts of the rustlers' Skinny Creek hideout was still a mystery.

"Tell me what this Tim fellow looks like," Ki asked, to keep Danny's mind off brooding. "I want to picture him in my mind, for when I kill him."

"Just looks like a cowpuncher," Danny sulked. "About six feet tall, and needs a shave. He's packing a Colt .38 in a waist-belt holster." The boy paused. "Is it true what they called you? You're a Chinaman?" But before Ki could reply, Danny exclaimed, "We're here! We're at Skinny Creek!"

"Tell me where we are going!" Ki hissed. "Whisper!"

"Well, you know that it's only one street," Danny began. "We're circling around to come in at the end where the hotel is."

Ki smiled grimly to himself. That would be the one-room flophouse that marked the edge of the town.

"We're coming up to a little shack built against the side of a hill. I'd say it's about a hundred yards behind the hotel. There's a lot of rocks and old timbers lying about."

Ki concentrated. "Yes, I remember the shack. But it is

so small. I thought it was merely a tool shed."

"Whatever it is, we're heading directly for it," Danny said. "Tim is unlocking the doors. Holy smoke! It's some kind of tunnel!"

Of course! Ki thought. His thoughts leaped back to his night of lovemaking with Mary Hudson, the widow who ran the general store:

"Skinny Creek wasn't always just a stopping place for cowhands passing through," she'd said. *It was an up-and-coming mining town . . . There was a silver mine operating . . .' Course, the vein petered out . . ."*

The vein had petered out, Ki scolded himself. Why had he not thought to ask where the mine was located?

"We're going right into a hole cut into the side of this here hill!" Danny said, awestruck. "Horses and all, we're just rolling right in. It's starting to get mighty dark," the boy complained. "One of 'em has just closed the doors. But there's kerosene lanterns strung along the ceiling up ahead."

Ki could smell the burning fuel, as well as the pungent odor of horse droppings. The rustlers evidently kept their mounts with them in the abandoned mine. That was why Ki had found no sign of their horses in the town's stable.

The samurai strained his weak eyes in an attempt to see the lanterns Danny had mentioned. Yes! There they were, above his head! His eyes *were* growing stronger! Ki felt like weeping with joy. To the rustlers and to Danny, the lanterns were bright enough to illuminate the mine tunnel. To Ki they were wavering, diffuse balls of fuzzy light. They reminded the samurai of the twinkling, nighttime sea creatures he used to watch rising up through the inky Japanese waters, when he himself was Danny's age. Given a few days to heal . . .

"We're stopping," Danny remarked. "We're in a big, hollowed-out cave."

"This is an old, abandoned silver mine," Ki told him. "Is there just one chamber?"

"That's all there is that I can see. But they do have a lot

of stacked crates and sacks of supplies. The piles are taller than a man."

A strange smile began to play at the corners of Ki's mouth. "They have brought us into an old mine. No sun ever penetrates here. This is the habitat of the mole . . ."

A mole can be quite a fierce fighter, Ki thought. *Even if he is blind . . .*

The dry flutter of leathery wings and a high-pitched squeak caught Ki's attention. He followed the bat's progress with his ears.

"I hate bats," Danny shuddered.

"The bat is a fine omen for us," Ki argued. "The blind bat becomes my brother."

One of the horses, frightened by the sudden swooping dive of the rodent, let out a nervous whinny. The other mounts picked up the fear, and soon there was a flurry of stamping hooves and nickering among the rustlers' horses. The outlaws calmed their mounts, and then continued to unsaddle them.

Danny noticed that Ki had cocked his head toward the noise. "They've got all of their horses in a rope corral up against the right wall, the way you're looking."

"I hear water."

Danny laughed. "Pretty good. I can *see* it, but I sure can't *hear* it. A stream must run through this hill we're in. Water is seeping through that same wall. They've built a trough beneath it for the horses, and for themselves, I reckon. They also got bales of hay stacked up. When they need more, I guess—"

"Tom Schiff sends over a wagonload," Ki finished for him. "And he sends over their supplies, and in exchange, he takes the cattle whose brands these men have altered, and adds them to his herd."

"Makes sense," Danny said. "Schiff's got such a large spread, nobody's going to notice a few dozen more cows added to it now and then."

"There is more at stake than a few dozen head of cattle," Ki began, but Danny cut him off.

"Shows what you know about ranching," the boy said angrily. "A few dozen head can make the difference between a profit and a loss on a spread the size of my pa's—I mean *mine,*" he corrected himself pointedly. "A small outfit can't afford to lose even one cow to a thief. We lose enough as it is to accidents and cold weather and coyotes—"

Danny grew silent as one of the rustlers came, to lead their horsedrawn buckboard deeper into the cavern.

"Unhitch the kid's horse, and put it in the corral," Tim ordered. "Tie the kid up the way you did the chink, and stick both of 'em up against those sacks of flour. They'll keep there till we figure out what to do with them."

"Take it easy, kid, I ain't gonna hurt you," one of the rustlers soothed as he bound the frightened boy's hands and feet, connecting his ropes to Ki's. Like Siamese twins, the two climbed awkwardly out of the wagon, to shuffle over to the flour sacks and then flop down.

"Damn," Danny muttered. He stared at the buckboard, now wheeled far out of reach. "I forgot about my rifle under the tent. I could have blasted them—"

"That is why I did not mention it," Ki said. "You would have managed to squeeze off only one shot before all seven of those professional shooters turned their pistols on us."

"I guess," Danny pouted. "Listen!"

The corralled horses once again began to act up. Ki heard the squeak of another bat, this one gliding far above the cavern floor. "The horses do not like it here," he said quietly.

"N-neither do I," Danny whined. "It's c-cold, and I'm afraid of those bats." He cringed against Ki's side as another bat flew across the cavern. "W-with my h-hands tied like this, they c-could g-get in m-my h-hair!"

"The bats will not hurt you. I told you that they are our friends."

"How do you figure t-that?" Danny pressed his face against Ki's bare arm, cringing again at the sound of flapping wings.

Ki felt the boy's tears running down his skin, and the

boy's wet lashes flicking like the feelers of tiny insects against his bicep. "Listen to me, Danny," Ki began, trying to talk the boy out of his fast-growing panic. "I have a riddle. Answer it for me. The bats bring us good news. Try and think what it is."

"I'm afraid—"

"I cannot see, Danny," Ki pretended to whimper. "You must help me puzzle out this riddle, for you are my eyes! Bats must hunt for their food," he offered as a hint.

"They hunt at night," Danny countered. "But they can't hunt in *here,* can they?" He grew excited. "You're saying that they hide in here during the day, but at night—"

"They leave this cavern to hunt *outside.*"

"But the doors we came through are closed."

"There is another way out, Danny," Ki declared. "The bats prove it to us each time they fly by. It is a good omen. You *are* going to live to carry on your father's name..." Ki felt the boy's eyes staring at him.

"Who are you, mister?" Danny asked plaintively. "I heard what those rustlers said before, when they tied you up. My pa didn't kill any of them, *you* did that. And I saw what you did to those Utes, and how you threw that knife at Tim, without even being able to *see* him. You do things other folks can only dream about. Who are you?"

"I am from a country called Japan. In my land I am known as a samurai."

"W-what's *that?*"

"A warrior. What you might call a gunslick," Ki smiled.

"Ki, you're one hell of a gunslick, then," Danny marveled. "Never heard of one before who could ply his trade while *blind.*" He yawned. "I'm getting mighty sleepy."

"Rest," Ki said. "Think on how you were once afraid of the bats, and how they are now your friends. Their wings will lead us to the way out of this cave."

"I wish my pa had been more like you," Danny murmured as he settled his head against one of the pillowlike flour sacks. "Then he'd still be alive..." The boy's breathing grew regular as he settled into sleep.

Ki's mind drifted back through the years, to that time in Japan when he was scarcely older than Danny. His training with his samurai teacher was coming to an end. *"Hirata,"* the adolescent apprentice had addressed his old master, *"my own family has forsaken me. You are my spiritual father . . ."*

Hirata, Ki now addressed the dead warrior, *is your* kami *hovering even here? Perhaps it rides on the back of a bat, the way you used to ride your feudal lord's warhorses. How you must be laughing in heaven! The wheel of* karma *has turned full around! Another orphan boy ripped too soon from childhood is in need of help. Could I fail him, and still face you when I die, teacher?*

Another bat flapped by. Ki watched it go, and sent his vow to ride its scaly wings to freedom. *The boy will live. I will send him out through the exit the bats use, and I will keep the rustlers from pursuing him. The only light in this cavern is that cast by the lanterns. I will extinguish that light and then, in the darkness, I will make this cavern a tomb for seven thieves—and perhaps for one blind samurai.*

Ki settled back to try and sleep. "I am sorry, Jessie," he whispered. "Just this once, I must put another before you. *Karma* has decreed it. This orphan boy shall live!"

Ki awoke to a presence he felt standing over him. "Who is there?" he whispered, not wanting to wake Danny.

"Don't you remember me?" a female voice asked in startled dismay.

It took him a moment to place the voice. It was Mary Hudson, the widow who ran the general store. "Forgive me, I did not mean to offend you," he said tenderly. "It is that—"

"Oh, my God!" Mary gasped. She crouched down to stare into Ki's face, noticing the scabbed cut on his forehead, and his staring eyes. *How they sparkled during that one night of lovemaking,* Mary thought. Now Ki's eyes were as dull and lifeless as broken bits of brown whiskey-bottle glass. "You're blind," she gasped. "Oh, *no*..."

Ki heard the catch in her voice. "Do not cry, woman!" he scolded. "There is no time for that. Tell me, are they listening to us?"

Mary shook her head, and then she remembered, and quickly said, "No. Those that aren't sleeping or eating are keeping an eye on us, but they can't hear us if we whisper. They've got no reason to listen. They don't know about... I mean, that we—"

"Of course," Ki said tenderly. "Though I cannot see you, Mary, I can picture your pale blue eyes and your black, black hair." He reached out his hand, and Mary guided it to her face. "You have your hair in a single plait down your back," Ki murmured.

"I'll loosen it for you," she whispered. "In bed. When you're out of here."

Ki did not answer, but asked, "What are *you* doing in here?"

"One of them came to fetch me. Said that they had a hurt man and a young boy, and that I was to bring proper vittles for both. They also told me you needed clothes." She glanced around to make sure no rustler was close enough to spy upon them. "They said that you were a chink," she said. "I sort of hoped that what they meant was Japanese."

"In my case, they usually do," Ki said wryly.

"That's why I brought you a special sort of flannel shirt," she whispered. "Just in case it *was* you. Lean forward."

Ki did as he was told, and felt her drape a shirt around his shoulders. Something hard was sewn inside the shirt. The shape of it pressing against his skin told him what it was. He had felt that shape many times before...

"The *shuriken* blade I left under your pillow," Ki said, remembering to keep his voice very soft. "Thank you, Mary!"

"I sewed it in as soon as they told me about you," she replied happily. "Only took me a minute to do. What's going on? Who's that boy?" As she talked, she set out a meal of soft white bread, cheese, and hot soup. The food's aroma woke Danny up. He smiled shyly at Mary as he dug into the meal.

As they ate, Ki filled Mary in on what had happened. When he was done telling their story, it was his turn to ask a question. "Have you always known that the rustlers were using this mine as their hideout?"

"I did," Mary replied, meanwhile daubing at the cut on Ki's forehead with a cloth dipped in soapy water. "So does the rest of Skinny Creek. I sell them supplies. The blacksmith cares for their horses, and so on. None of us much like it, but there ain't a hell of a lot we can do about it. We've got no law, and no menfolk handy enough with a gun to drive these gunslicks away."

"You didn't tell me where they were hiding," Ki reproached her.

"You did not ask me!" Mary said defiantly. "It seems like you didn't see fit to trust me, back then!"

Ki nodded. "I indeed deserve my present blindness, for being so blind earlier," he said ruefully.

"Now don't you go saying that," Mary sniffled. "I'd give you a kiss and a hug, if I wasn't worried that one of these jaspers would catch me at it and start wondering what was going on. You see, a few of them have already tried to get close to me, and have found out that I ain't usually the kissing kind!"

"Mary, listen carefully. I have a plan to free the boy. When I do, I want you to take care of him. Defend him until you can get him back to Nettle Grove."

"I ain't leaving without you," Danny interrupted, his mouth full of bread and cheese.

"That's right, he ain't," Mary said adamantly.

"Both of you do as I say!" Ki seethed.

"And who are you to order a woman like me around?" Mary hissed. "*You* are going to do as *I* say, else I'll tell them you mean to escape, and take back that there little knife of yours, just to keep your fool self alive a bit longer!"

Danny had listened, fascinated, to the exchange. "Ki, you beat the Utes, and you beat the rustlers, but I think you just met your match."

"Now *there*'s a smart young fella," she smiled, patting his cheek. "What's your name, son?"

"Danny, ma'am."

"Call me Mary. Take care of this man for me, Danny. He's right handsome, and can fight fierce, but sometimes he's so darned stubborn . . ."

"Yes, ma'am—I mean, Mary," Danny smiled. "Don't worry. I won't let nothing happen to Ki."

"Good boy!" Mary gazed at him. "You know, my own boy, Lord rest his soul, would be about your age now."

"This is all quite touching," Ki grumbled.

"Quit your sassing!" Mary laughed. "You're just in a tizzy 'cause you know I'm right. It's almost sundown, which means you'd be up against seven men. Tomorrow they're sending some riders west, to tell the man they work for about you. You might only be up against three or four of them *then,* now wouldn't that be better?"

Ki sat stoically silent, determined to ignore her.

"Wouldn't it?" Mary repeated. Her fingers reached under the shirt, purposely tickling his nipples before settling—as if in warning—upon the *shuriken* sewn to the flannel. "Well?" she asked in a stern, threatening tone.

"Yes it would be better," Ki fairly snarled. But he was forced to admit to himself that she was indeed right.

"Stubborn as the day is long," Mary clucked lovingly as she tugged the shirt closer around his broad shoulders.

"If my hands were not tied," Ki seethed, "do you know what I would do to you?"

"Well," she grinned, "if you ever run out of ideas, I got a few of my own on the subject. But never mind that now. The boy here is drinking this all in. Little pitchers got big ears, you know . . ." She looked over her shoulder. "Uh-oh! They're coming to fetch me. My time here is up. Don't do a thing until you hear from me! Please! Trust me! I've got a few tricks up my sleeve!"

Ki listened to her boots echoing as she hurried away.
"Lord, she was pretty!" Danny breathed.
Ki smiled. "I told you that you would learn to appreciate women."

★

Chapter 9

It was getting on toward sundown when Jessie left her hotel and made her way to the marshal's office. There was a large crowd standing around outside Forbes's door. Jessie craned her neck to see, by the bright illumination of lanterns, a hand-lettered poster calling for volunteers to assemble at the stables at daybreak. At that time, horses would be lent free of charge, so that a search party could be formed to try and find Daniel Tang.

As Jessie listened to the crowd buzzing about the murder of Hiram Tang, she spotted Tom Schiff, flanked by a couple of his drovers, standing on the plankwalk. The silvery conchos on the cattleman-banker's Stetson glittered in the lanternlight as he stepped aside to make room for Marshal Forbes, who was just then coming out of his office. Following Forbes was Deputy Stills and another lawman, a bearded fellow who Jessie had seen patrolling the township.

"All right! Settle down and listen!" Forbes shouted. "You all know what happened to Hiram Tang. We figure it was them Utes that did it. His boy is missing, and we aim to find some sign of young Daniel."

"Can I say something, Marshal?" Schiff asked.

"Go right ahead, Tom," Forbes said politely.

"Folks!" Schiff began loudly. "I just want you to know that despite my disagreements with Hiram Tang, I'm powerful sorry that he died the way he did. Tomorrow at dawn, me and my boys here are riding back to my spread. From there, we aim to search in the general direction of Skinny Creek—"

"Hold on!" Deputy Stills interrupted suddenly.

"What is it, young man?" Schiff glowered.

"I don't cotton to you claiming to search Skinny Creek all by your lonesome, *that's* what it is," Stills drawled.

"Settle down, Hank," Forbes warned.

"Settle down nothing, Marshal!" Stills shouted. "Miss Starbuck says her missing friend tracked them rustlers to Skinny Creek—"

"Don't you start on that rustler nonsense," Forbes literally screamed in rage, while Schiff looked on approvingly. Jessie, along with the rest of the crowd, stood watching and listening in shocked silence. "If Mr. Schiff says he's going to search Skinny Creek, he's going to do it!"

"Maybe I'll just ride along with him, then," Stills said.

"That's not necessary, Marshal," Schiff said hastily.

"You heard the man," Forbes told his deputy. "You'll ride with our search party tomorrow—"

"Like hell I will!" Stills thundered.

"You'll do as I say, or else turn in your badge!" Forbes countered.

"Come on now, Cal," the bearded deputy suddenly broke in. "Hank," he soothed, looking from one man to the other. "You two have been together for an awful long time."

"Keep out of this, Oakley," Forbes warned. "Hank, you obey my orders or you're out of your job!"

"Hank's been your head deputy for two years now," the bearded lawman tried again.

"Forget it, Oakley," Stills said disgustedly.

The tall, blond deputy unpinned the badge from his

leather vest and tossed it to Forbes. "I'm through," he announced. He turned to stride away, but found his path blocked by one of Schiff's men. The drover had sauntered around the edge of the crowd to get behind Stills during his shouting match with his superior.

"Guess you went too far this time," the drover laughed in Stills's face. He was a big man, dressed, like his employer, in a corduroy suit.

"Get out of my way," Stills said quietly.

"Don't think so," the man said. "Not until you apologize nice and loud to my boss, Mr. Schiff. You've run me in for being drunk too many times for me to let you off easy, Stills. Now apologize!"

"I ain't gonna tell you again. Get out of my way!"

"Apologize to Mr. Schiff!" The drover stepped away from Stills, at the same time brushing back his coattails to reveal a brace of nickel-plated pistols in a cross-draw rig.

Jessie, watching, began to fear for Stills. The drover confronting him was no cowboy at all, but a professional gunslick. Cowpunchers didn't wear suits, and they didn't carry glittery double pistols. She looked to Marshal Forbes to put a stop to this showdown, but he was too busy signing up men for tomorrow's search party to even notice that Stills was in trouble.

The drover reached out with his left hand to poke Stills in the chest. "You'd better do as I say. You ain't got your badge to hide behind anymore." The man's right hand hovered over his pistol as he spat, "You've turned in your star for a chance at that Texas slut!"

Before the drover could say another word, Stills moved in on him. The deputy kept his hands open and at his sides, in a wrestler's stance. The drover was a fast draw, but Stills was quicker. He batted the man's shiny gun out of the way with his left hand, and then brought his right fist through to slam the fellow in the belly. The drover doubled over. Stills brought his left fist around in a short, hard cross, catching the man on his jaw, just beneath the ear. At the same time, Stills swiveled around on one leg to plant his left boot toe square against the seat of the drover's corduroy trousers. Howling, the man belly-flopped to the ground. He skidded several feet, his nose ploughing a furrow in the street.

"Jerk," Stills muttered as he turned away.

The drover flipped over onto his back. Blood was streaming from the great, raw patches scraped off his nose and lips. His fine suit, like his face, had been torn by his skid. He roared in pain and fury as his left hand clawed for the grips of his remaining pistol, for a chance at Stills's back.

Jessie was about to haul out her own Colt, but the marshal beat them both to the draw. His hogleg thundered fire and smoke, and a clot of earth kicked up beside the fallen drover. Stills spun around in a crouch, his own .44 appearing in his hand as fast as lightning.

The drover, covered now from behind as well as in front, suddenly thought better of drawing. "He started it!" he shouted, choking back his frustration as he pointed a quivering finger at Stills.

"Ain't you gonna arrest that gunslick?" Stills drawled as he holstered his revolver.

"I see no reason for charges against my man," Schiff broke in. "He was just trying to protect me, Marshal."

"All right, then, Mr. Schiff," Forbes agreed meekly.

"Forbes!" Stills shouted. "You're hopeless."

"I want you out of my jurisdiction!" Forbes hotly replied.

Jessie watched the marshal glare at Stills as the ex-deputy walked away. She ran to catch up with him, but before she could say a word, Stills winked at her.

"Y-you mean that was all an act?" she stammered. "You and Forbes had it all planned?"

"All except for Oakley trying to smooth things over, and that dumb gunslick making a play," Stills admitted. "We sort of had to improvise once they got into the act." His laughing eyes grew serious. "I am sorry for what that gunslick called you, Jessie."

"Not as sorry as you made him, I suspect," she smiled, slipping her arm through his as they strolled along in the gathering twilight. "You never told me you were Forbes's head deputy," she began.

"Never took to blowing my own horn," Stills said. "Anyway, the fact that I *am* the head deputy is the reason why we had to set up this little bluff," he confided. "It'd look mighty suspicious if I didn't go along with Marshal Forbes tomorrow on that wild-goose chase Schiff's sending him on, unless I was no longer working for him.

"What are we going to do tomorrow?" Jessie asked, looking up at Stills as he drew her closer by slipping his arm around her shoulder.

"Tomorrow we ride to Skinny Creek, to make our own little search. We should get there hours before Schiff. He's got to stop off at his spread to round up some of his men." The deputy grinned at Jessie, displaying his sparkling white teeth. "It's *tonight* that's going to take the cake, girl!" He dug into the pocket of his worn jeans and came up with a ring of keys.

"What are they for?" Jessie asked, totally befuddled both by what Stills was saying, and the way his fingers were absently tickling their way up and down her spine. Stills's touch upon her, even through the layers of her clothing, was arousing.

The deputy nuzzled her hair. "Lord, you smell good," he sighed happily, pulling her close for an embrace.

"But what are they for?" Jessie breathed.

"What?" Stills mumbled.

"The keys," Jessie said, pulling slightly away.

"Oh!" Stills chuckled. "I swear, having you close to me makes me as absent-minded as if I'd drunk a pint of rye. These here are the keys to Schiff's bank."

"What?" Jessie exclaimed. "How'd you get them?"

"Town marshal has got to be able to get into the bank in case there's a fire or a robbery or something."

"Does Forbes know you have them?" Jessie demanded, her eyes sparkling with mischief.

"'Course he does," Stills replied. "He gave them to me. This is all his idea. He figures that maybe we can find some of that evidence linking Schiff with those Prussian foreigners in the bank's files."

"He's wonderful!" Jessie gushed.

"Simmer down now," Stills said sternly. "You've got to realize that if we get caught doing this, Forbes is going to have to claim that I took these keys on my own. Anyhow, maybe you'd better not come along tonight—"

"Not a chance I'm going to let you do this alone," Jessie cut him off.

"Now think about it—" Stills began, but Jessie smothered the rest of what he was about to say with a kiss.

"I never properly thanked you for defending my honor just now," she whispered, planting more kisses along the strong line of his jaw. "You're very fast with your fists, and quick on the draw . . ."

Stills's hands reached beneath Jessie's jacket to fondle her firm, warm breasts. "Fast with my fists?" he mumbled thickly, thinking about how Jessie's blouse was so wonderfully satiny, and the fabric was so sheer that he could feel her nipples hardening beneath the silk. "Well, I don't like to blow my own horn—"

"Yes, you said that," Jessie whispered, at the same time as she licked at his ear. "Maybe later I'll blow it for you."

"Yes, ma'am," Stills chuckled.

"If we're caught, do you think we could be put in the same cell?" she asked.

"Well, ma'am, I do have some contacts in the marshal's office." His fingers glided down to explore the sassy swell of her bottom. "It's just dark. We've got some time before—"

"Who's over there?" a spinsterish female voice called from out of the shadows.

Both Jessie and Stills instinctively pulled away from each other, giggling like schoolchildren caught in some naughty act.

The deputy winked. "I'll meet you outside your hotel in about an hour. Town will be quiet by then."

He glided silently away, leaving Jessie standing alone

with a thumping heart and a pair of jeans that had suddenly become quite itchy, and about two sizes too small . . .

An hour later, Jessie was standing outside her hotel when a flaring match attracted her attention. She followed the tiny flame until it fizzled out, to find Stills waiting for her at the mouth of an alley that ran alongside the hotel.

"We're gonna come around to the rear of the bank," Stills told her as they walked past garbage bins and outhouses. "There's a night watchman. An old fellow—"

"Is he in on what we're doing?" Jessie asked.

"Nope. That's why you've got to be real quiet. That old codger is true-blue honest. He's gonna do his best to shoot us when we go in." Stills smiled to reassure her. "Course, he *ain't* gonna shoot us, but just the same, I want to put him out of commission as gently as possible."

The bank's back door was a solid wooden affair with wire mesh protecting the tiny glass window set at eye level. The lock was protected by a metal plate, but there was no protection against the right key. The mechanism clicked smoothly, and the heavy door swung open without a sound.

Stills put a finger to his lips, and stepped through the door. Jessie followed close behind. She noticed that Stills had not drawn his gun. He was obviously serious about not harming the watchman, even if it meant risking his own life.

A gentle hand on her shoulder told her that the deputy wanted her to stay put. She watched Stills slip off into the shadows, and was at once reminded of Ki. Like the samurai, the deputy had a spooky way of moving very quickly.

"Who's there?" came a rusty, elderly voice. "Speak up! I got me a gun!"

From where Jessie was hiding, she could see the night watchman's shadowy form. Looming up behind the man was Stills. She watched the deputy clamp one hand over the watchman's gun to keep it from firing, and the other hand move to cover the fellow's mouth. The watchman moaned once and crumpled, and Stills caught the sagging body in his arms and gently lowered it to the floor.

"I don't think I hurt him," the deputy muttered as Jessie came over. "You've got to be careful with old geezers like this. They've got mighty brittle bones."

"What did you do to him?" she asked.

"Just a little trick I know," he replied. "The old fellow ought to be out for a while."

Stills lit a nearby table lamp, turning the flame very low. As the shadows retreated to the far corners, Jessie saw that they were behind the tellers' cages.

"This way," Stills said, holding the lamp like a torch. Schiff's office is back here."

He led her to a door with a frosted glass panel written, in gilt script, THOMAS SCHIFF, PRESIDENT. That door was locked as well, but Stills found the right key to open it on the ring given to him by Marshal Forbes.

Schiff's offices had oak wainscoting on the lower portions of the walls. Lemon-yellow paint picked up where the paneling left off. The floor was carpeted in red wool. There was a large, tanned calfskin tacked to the wall behind Schiff's desk. Tooled into the hide was the message: *To Tom, with Best Wishes for Success from the Nettle Grove Cattlemen's Association.* Burnt into the skin, beneath the inscription, were the various brands of the member spreads.

"He's president of that too," Stills said dryly. "Folks reckon that if he lives long enough, he'll be Wyoming's first senator, come statehood."

"Can you imagine having a senator who owes his first allegiance to a foreign power?" Jessie shuddered. "That's what makes it all the more important that we stop him now." She tried the desk's drawers. "They're locked. I don't suppose you've got the keys to his desk on that ring?"

"Now that's asking right much, ma'am," Stills laughed. "We'll have to pick 'em open." He dug a pocket knife out of his jeans. One blade had been filed toothpick-thin.

Jessie waited patiently as he fiddled each lock open. She then rifled through the opened drawer's contents as the deputy went on to the next lock. She found various files, deeds, and ledgers, but nothing that had anything to do with Schiff's deal with the Prussians.

When they were done, Stills shook his head. "Well, it was a nice try on our part, but—"

"Hold on," Jessie said. "There have got to be more files than these in the bank."

"Well . . ." Stills removed his Stetson to scratch at his blond curls. "I reckon they've got lots of deeds and such in the vault, but why would Schiff mix his personal business in with papers any damn clerk could stumble across?"

"Because the safest place to hide an incriminating contract or agreement would be in a mountain of paper!" Jessie exclaimed.

"The vault, eh?" Stills's big brown eyes grew thoughtful, then he grinned at Jessie. "Is this more of your feminine intuition?"

"Reckon so," she drawled, in a precise parody of Stills's own down-home manner. "Let's us mosey over and take us a peek at that there vault."

"We've got just one problem," Stills mused as he guided their way out of Schiff's office and back toward the tellers' area, finding his way by the dim light of the sputtering lamp.

"What would that be?" Jessie asked innocently.

"The vault will be locked, I don't have the key to it, and while I'm right smug about my ability with desk drawers"— Stills paused to turn up the lamp— "I ain't gonna be opening *that* with my penknife."

The lamp's reflection danced across the shiny steel surface of the vault's massive door. Thick reinforcing bars crisscrossed the door, like the muscles that might bulge beneath the skin of a giant's chest. Set in the door's middle was a saucer-sized combination dial. Beneath that was a lever to pull the door open.

"Hmm," Jessie mused. She regarded the vault with her hands on her hips. "I don't suppose they might have forgotten to lock it this time?"

"We could knock," Stills suggested. "Maybe a couple of sacks of money will hop over and let us in."

"You're sure you can't open it?" Jessie asked him.

"Hey, now!" Stills griped. "I ain't a safecracker, I'm a lawman!"

"And an absolutely marvelous one, at that," Jessie smiled. She took off her Stetson and pulled back her long mane of hair, quickly binding it with a length of string taken from a teller's cage nearby. "Would you fetch me one of those drinking glasses in Schiff's office? They're next to the water carafe on his desk."

"I know where they are," Stills muttered to himself as he went to do her bidding. "Hell of a time to get thirsty."

"No! Bring it empty!" she laughed.

Stills returned with the glass. "What do you want it empty for?"

"You'll see," Jessie knelt down before the vault's door. She pressed the open mouth of the glass against the steel, just above the dial, and pressed her ear against the bottom. She began slowly to turn the dial, one click at a time.

"I don't believe it!" Stills gasped. "Don't tell me you can actually figure out the combination that way?"

"I can hear the tumblers falling when I—there! That's the first one," Jessie said triumphantly.

"I don't believe it," Stills repeated weakly. "But you didn't know how to pick the desk locks?"

"Of course I did," she chided him mildly. "Ah! There's the second number. I could have had those drawers open in about a third of the time, I might add."

"Then why'd you let me do it?" Stills demanded.

Jessie smiled up at him, as sweet as honey. "Just because a woman can do certain things better than a man, doesn't mean she really wants to." She lowered the glass for a moment. "Ki taught me this particular trick. There's no lock ever devised that *he* can't open in seconds," she boasted. "But I've always had a natural talent for this kind of thing." She shrugged out of her denim jacket and went back to work.

Stills watched the tails of her silk blouse rise up out of the waistband of her jeans as she leaned forward to press her ear against the glass. Kneeling like that, with her back muscles stretched and straining, the deputy could not help gazing at her pear-shaped bottom.

"I first learned how to pick locks when I was at finishing school back East."

"Don't tell me they teach such things to young girls!" Stills exclaimed.

"Don't be such a silly," Jessie murmured absently, her concentration focused on the tiny noises of the turning tumblers. "The headmistress kept the school's supply of apricot brandy locked up in a cupboard. We all took turns trying to open it, and it turned out that I had the best feel." She giggled. "That made me a very popular girl, late at night," she continued. "We'd all sneak down to the parlor in our nighties, and I'd take a hatpin and—"

"Ain't childhood grand?" Stills smirked.

"*Mine* was," Jessie said smugly. "There! I got it!" She lowered the glass, took hold of the vault door handle, and turned it. "Turns free . . ." she said hopefully, climbing up to her feet. She pulled, and the vault door swung open.

"Easy as pie," Jessie gloated, stepping into the vault. Stills followed, bringing the lamp. "Be careful it doesn't swing closed behind us," Jessie warned.

"Don't worry, it's counterbalanced," Stills told her, grateful that there was *something* this lovely little bundle of tricks didn't already know.

"Where do we start?" Jessie wondered out loud. The vault was about eight feet deep and six feet high.

Floor-to-ceiling shelves were filled with sacks of money. One section of shelving was stacked with brick-sized blocks of silver certificates, bound with elastic.

Stills was oblivious. He kept staring at the stacks of money.

"Hey," Jessie chuckled. "Don't forget, you're a lawman."

"I knew I picked the wrong line of work," he groaned.

"I'll never have *this* chance again."

"That's true." Jessie set to work going through the wooden file cabinet at the rear of the vault. "For one thing, you can't open this thing without me."

"Mostly I was thinking that a township like Nettle Grove rarely sees this much money at one time." He noticed that Jessie had pulled a thin folder out of the file and was reading it's contents. He approached with the lamp to give her more light. "I happen to know that most of this cash"—he gestured toward the wall of silver certificates—"belongs to the Cattlemen's Association. They've put together funds to buy some new breeding stock—"

Suddenly, Jessie waved the file folder in the air like a triumphant battle flag. "I found it!" she laughed delightedly. "It was filed under 'Schiff,' along with lots of other business papers and contracts for the delivery of cattle."

"Right where it was supposed to be," Stills mused.

"And where no one would think to look for it," Jessie added. "It's like that story Poe wrote about the letter hidden from the police. The character in the story stuck it in with lots of other correspondence in a letter box displayed in plain sight. The police considered the letter box so obvious a hiding place that they never thought to look there."

"Right!" Stills smiled. "'Course, this here vault ain't a letter box, but the basic idea is the same. Anybody who is *supposed* to be in here would work for Schiff, and an employee who wants to keep his job ain't gonna go poking around his boss's private papers."

"This contract is all the evidence Forbes will need!" Jessie scanned the pages. "Schiff sold the Prussians Hiram Tang's mineral rights in exchange for fifty thousand in cash. In other words, he sold what he didn't own."

"Holy smoke!" Stills's mouth dropped open. "Schiff was already one of the richest men in Wyoming Territory. Fifty thousand dollars would just about double his worth!"

Jessie looked up at the deputy. "I'll bet most of this paper money belongs to Schiff himself!" She ran over to Stills and gave him a big hug. "Hank! We've got Schiff dead to rights! This gives us his motive for trying to force Hiram Tang out of business. Now Forbes can investigate the entire matter without fear of Schiff taking away his badge. The town has got to stop dancing to Schiff's tune, now that we can prove he's committed at least one fraud."

Stills nodded. "It sure does make old Tom the prime suspect in Hiram's murder." The deputy's eyes narrowed. "But Schiff could still weasel out of this. We've got to locate Danny before Schiff does, else the boy is a goner for sure!"

The lawman realized that he had Jessie in his arms. "But we can't start searching for Danny—"

"And Ki," Jessie reminded him, hugging him tighter.

"And Ki, of course," Stills promised. "But we can't start until tomorrow. Tonight, let's celebrate, starting with a kiss."

Jessie's lips on his were like a cool drink of water to a man lost in a desert. Their tongues intertwined, to do a mating dance in time to the one their bodies were just now grinding out. When they finally broke apart, Jessie's eyes were twin, huge, round, green pools of surprise and delight.

"Lord," she breathed, as a lovely shade of pink colored her cheeks. "Hank Stills! Where did you ever learn to kiss like *that?*"

"I figure anything worth doing is worth concentrating on," Stills replied. Locking his arms around Jessie, he picked her up and cartwheeled her around.

"Set me down!" Jessie squealed, her legs flailing the air.

"Uh-oh! Look out!" Stills laughed. He tried to slow his spin, but it was too late. Jessie's boots hit some of the stacks of paper money.

The wall of bills swayed back and forth, and then toppled forward. The bricks of silver certificates burst their elastic binding as they hit the floor. Money fanned out in a wall-to-wall carpet across the vault.

Jessie and Stills could only watch and laugh. They held their sides and doubled up, giggling until the tears streamed from their eyes.

"It's raining greenbacks!" Stills crowed. He scooped up a handful of bills and tossed them into the air. The silver certificates wafted down like summer leaves stripped from a tree.

"Just look at it," Jessie sighed. "It's, it's—"

"It's a haypile of money," Stills offered.

She nodded. "A *bed* of it."

Their eyes locked. They didn't need words to exchange their thoughts.

Jessie slowly began to unbutton her silk blouse. "This is just plain loco," she whispered.

"The watchman might wake up," Stills nodded. He unhitched his gunbelt, letting it fall to the floor.

"If we're caught doing this..." Jessie shucked off her blouse. Her nipples rose in anticipation. "If we do this..."

"If we *don't* do it, we'll never forgive ourselves," Stills insisted. He'd already kicked off his worn boots, and now peeled down his faded denims. He wore no underwear. His erection was hard enough to fairly poke a hole right through the vault's steel door.

Jessie watched it bob up and down like the handle of a pump. She discarded her boots, gun, and jeans while Stills removed the rest of his clothes. A moment later they were rolling and tumbling upon the pile of money. The paper bills quickly lost their crispness beneath their bodies. The certificates slipped over and under them like fresh green grass as they burrowed into it like playful puppies.

Stills caught Jessie around the waist, and pulled her, stomach down, across his lap. He fingered the scant undergarment she was wearing. It was made of silk and edged with lace. "I'm no virgin, ma'am, but what the hell are these things?" Stills drawled. "I ain't never seen the likes of them before." He ran his hands across the silk-covered mounds of her behind. "Why, they hardly cover your rump!"

"Oh, they're nothing much," Jessie laughed. "Just something I ordered from Paris. You can't expect me to wear a pair of bulky pantaloons beneath my tight jeans?"

"Why wear anything at all?" Stills asked as he peeled

off the scrap of silk and tossed it to where her other clothes lay piled in a corner. "There, that's lots better." He tickled the tufts of blonde fur poking out from between Jessie's legs.

"Going without some sort of knickers is all right for a man," she began, meanwhile stroking Stills's hardness until it bucked like a bronco against her lower belly. "But a woman has got to have a little something extra between that hard leather saddle and that tenderness between her legs . . ."

Stills flipped her over. "Guess *I* got a little something extra for that tenderness between your legs," he said fervidly. He began to swirl his tongue around the pink aureoles of her nipples.

Jessie parted her legs. She was already soaking wet. She drew Stills into her, opening up for him the way a sunflower's blossom will spread at the first rays of dawn. "Oh, God!" she moaned.

Stills smiled down into her fever-bright eyes. He kissed her tenderly as he rose and dipped in a slow, steady rhythm. "Reckon you're inspiring me, Jessie," he crooned. He patted the soft carpet of paper money in which they were nested. "*Something* is, at any rate!" he chuckled. "Nothing gets a man's sap rising like cold cash or a warm woman!"

Moaning, Jessie twisted and writhed as Stills drove into her with movements that—for all of their control—contained the power of a steam locomotive. The deputy's tight, muscular body was sheened with sweat. His brown eyes glittered in the lamplight. Jessie began to feel her orgasm building inside her.

She kicked her long legs straight up into the air, and then clamped her velvet-smooth thighs around Stills's bucking hips.

Just as her own climax exploded inside her, Stills arched his back and spurted into her. His eyes screwed shut, and his mouth opened wide as he howled like a wolf baying at the moon.

"H-hush," Jessie managed to gasp as her fingers tickled up his spine. "*Ohhhh!*" she sang as a shuddery aftershock of feeling flowed through her.

"Hush yourself!" Stills said merrily.

"It's just that I'm worried that we've alerted the entire town," Jessie laughed.

"Vault's soundproof, I reckon," Stills drawled as he slipped out of her. He cradled Jessie in his arms and rested his cheek against her hair.

"That was wonderful," Jessie said contentedly.

"Just goes to show you that money ain't everything," he smirked.

"But it helps," Jessie chuckled. She moved out of his arms and rose up on her knees to stretch. As she did, Stills burst out laughing. "What?" Jessie asked, startled. The deputy could only point at her rump.

Jessie looked at herself over her shoulder. A solid layer of silver certificates had plastered themselves to the lush, round cheeks of her perspiration-damp backside. Every inch was covered. Jessie gave an experimental little wiggle, but the bills held fast. "I guess I've been tarred and feathered with money," she giggled.

"Reckon I've just had what every man dreams of," Stills said.

"What's that?"

He slapped her right smack on a twenty. "A million-dollar piece of ass!"

Jessie attacked him. He fell back as she straddled his belly to stick bills across his chest and down the rippling length of his torso. He soon grew hard again, and Jessie lifted herself just enough to guide him inside her. This time she rode the deputy like a horse, bending over him so that he could fondle her breasts. Knowing that this time would have to be their last, they tried their best to prolong their pleasure. The deputy met every fiery thrust with one of his own, until they'd crested their passion's hill, and began to roll uncontrollably down its incline.

This time when they came, their orgasms were gentle. Jessie locked her lips against his. They did not shout, but only breathed their moans into each other's mouths. Their tongues dueled like fencers as their interlaced bodies surrendered to bolts of pulsing feeling.

Just before she pulled herself free, Jessie scooped up two big double handfuls of bills and tossed them into the air. They shared one last kiss beneath a drenching spring shower of verdant money.

"Do you suppose we should, um, clean up?" Jessie asked as she finished dressing.

Stills surveyed the mess inside the vault as he tied his red bandanna around his throat. "We'd never be able to put it all back the way it was," he reasoned.

"True. And besides"—Jessie shrugged elaborately—"it *is* only money."

"Fifty thousand or more, you said, right?" Stills asked as he picked up the lamp.

"Right." Jessie folded the incriminating contract in half the long way, and thrust it through her gunbelt like a dagger.

"Well then," Stills said. "That settles it." He gestured toward the sodden pile of cash mounded on the floor. "I can plumb forget about tidying up. If it's *that* much money, this is one bed I'm never going to make!"

★

Chapter 10

Jessie shut and locked the bank vault on Stills's instructions. He wanted things to look natural for as long as possible, come tomorrow morning's opening.

On their way toward the back door, Stills paused to check on the unconscious night watchman. The old fellow was snoring peacefully. Stills knelt to check his pulse.

"He'll probably sleep till morning," the deputy grinned. He tucked the guard's old pistol—a percussion-cap revolver left over from the Civil War, but remodeled to take brass cartridges—back into its holster. Next, Stills lifted the slumbering man as easily as a child, and carried him over to a straight-backed chair.

"When he wakes up, he'll look around, see that everything is all right, and figure he dreamt it all," Stills chuckled as he artfully arranged the man into a sitting position.

"Actually, there's no way they can suspect a break-in," Jessie said as they left the bank. "We didn't take any money."

"Not a penny," Stills agreed as he locked the back door.

"The document we took won't be missed until it's too late to do Schiff any good, and those stacks of bills were so high that they could have fallen over on their own."

Jessie nodded silently as they walked back toward Main Street. Stills thought she seemed a bit melancholy.

"Hey," he called softly, taking hold of her arm and turning her around. "What's wrong?"

"Nothing," Jessie shrugged. She offered him a wistful little smile.

"It hasn't got anything to do with our lovemaking, has it?" the deputy asked, his brown eyes wide and serious.

Jessie hugged him. "No, I'm sorry. I guess I'd better tell you. I'm a bit upset by the fact that we *did* steal something."

"You mean the contract?" Stills asked as they resumed walking.

"Yes. I know that we did it for a good cause. But the Prussians probably think that what *they're* doing is for a good cause."

"Just you hold on there!" Stills shook his head. "That fancy school may have taught you about silk undies and lock-picking, but evidently not a hell of a lot about morality. Now I'm a lawman, but if I have to bend a little law in order to enforce a bigger one, that's just fine with me."

"But then what's the difference between us and Schiff?" Jessie frowned.

"The difference is that we're not hurting anybody, and that we're trying to stop someone who *has* hurt somebody. We suspect Schiff of causing Tang's murder by paying gunslicks to steal cows and shoot anyone who gets in their way while they're doing it."

"But—"

"But nothing, woman!" Stills scowled. "It's bad enough that a lawman has got to kiss the ass of every bigwig in town! That's what poor old Cal Forbes has got to do. Lord help us if this country ever gets to the point where a lawman can be stopped by a lot of petty little laws that an outlaw can hide behind."

Jessie gave his hand an affectionate squeeze. "You talk

like you've done a lot of thinking on this subject."

"Well, I like to read, and I've got my opinions on things..."

"I know, I know," Jessie giggled. "Anyway, thanks for cheering me up."

"My pleasure, ma'am." He pulled her close for a final hug before they left the alley for Main Street. "My rooming house is a few blocks down, just behind the blacksmith's shop. I gave Forbes the key to my room when he gave me these keys to the bank. The plan calls for me to meet with him and turn over any evidence we might have found."

"Then what?" Jessie asked.

"I figure the marshal will take one look at this contract and decide to come with us to Skinny Creek tomorrow. I reckon that a true-blue marshal backed up by a posse will be enough to convince Skinny Creek's citizens that it's safe to speak up about trouble in their vicinity."

"You think that the honest folks in Skinny Creek are in on it?" Jessie asked dubiously.

"Not in on it," Stills chuckled. "But scared of it. Where there's no law, badmen do what they please. There's damn few law-abiding citizens who know enough about using a gun to stand up to a professional badman. Right now, the citizens of Skinny Creek most likely feel like a dog with fleas. They're itching something awful, but they don't know what to do about it."

At the blacksmith's shop they turned right off Main Street. They were about halfway down the block when Stills muttered, "Uh-oh!" and pulled Jessie back into a shadowy doorway.

"What's wrong?"

"Remember that bearded deputy? Fella named Oakley? Well, he's waiting out in front of my rooming house."

"Maybe he came with Marshal Forbes," Jessie suggested.

"No," Stills grumbled. "Don't forget, he doesn't know anything about that phony shouting match Forbes and I acted out. Oakley thinks I'm really fired. Besides, if he knew Forbes was up there, why would he be waiting outside?"

"Do you think there's something wrong?" Jessie asked, worried.

"Not at all," Stills smiled. "Oakley's a good old sort. He's probably feeling bad about me quitting, and wants to commiserate." Stills pondered the situation. "His being there does complicate things. Tell you what. Better give me that contract now. I don't want Oakley to see it changing hands between us." Jessie handed him the document and watched him bend to tuck it into his boot, beneath his pants leg.

"There's one last problem," he confided as they resumed their walk. "You're gonna have to wait outside and talk to Oakley for a few minutes, at least until Forbes and I come down." Stills was apologetic. "You see, my landlady doesn't allow boarders to entertain females up in their rooms."

"Hello, Hank. Miss Starbuck, ma'am," Oakley greeted them both, doffing his broken-down Stetson in Jessie's direction. He was leaning against the gate of a white picket fence that surrounded the four-story rooming house. "I was making my rounds, and I thought I'd stop by to see how you was making out."

"Right nice of you," Stills said agreeably. "I take it you didn't go up to my room?"

"Nope. You still live on the fourth floor, right?" Oakley asked, and when Stills nodded, he said, "I came from the alley around the corner, so I could see that your window was dark."

Oakley beamed with pleasure over his detective work. He was a slender man of medium height, dressed in snug, rust-colored tweed trousers and a mismatched suit jacket of worn gray gabardine. An army flap holster rode his right thigh, suspended from a sagging leather garrison belt. The shiny brass star pinned to his faded lapel looked totally out of place.

Stills peered at Oakley until the man began to fidget. "You were never much of a poker player, mister. What's on your mind?"

Jessie watched the shabby, rumpled deputy shrug. Oakley's beard began just below his eyes, and fanned out into a brown bush that obscured the bottom portion of his face, so Jessie could not tell from his expression whether or not he was truly upset about something. Oakley's coal-black eyes did seem a trifle harried. . . .

"'Fess up now," Stills coaxed. "Say, Forbes hasn't gone and given you my job as head deputy?" he asked goodnaturedly.

"Just temporarily," Oakley admitted. He looked down at his muddy work shoes. "Cal says he ain't sure about my appointment just yet." He glanced at Jessie and then shifted his sad gaze to Stills. "Hank, getting the job this way don't give me pleasure, I want'cha to know that."

"Hey," Stills comforted. "Don't you fret. Things ain't as bad as they might seem . . ."

Oakley nodded, once again looking away. Stills took the opportunity to wink at Jessie. "Oakley, would you mind chatting here with Miss Starbuck for a few minutes? There's something I've got to do up in my room."

Oakley stood aside as Stills unhitched the gate. A kerosene lantern hanging from a post illuminated the flagstone walk. The bearded deputy and Jessie watched Stills climb the steps to the porch and disappear through the front door of the house.

Oakley leaned back against the gate. For a moment he seemed to be listening to the moths batting themselves against the lantern. "Sorry thing, what's happened 'tween the marshal and Hank," he finally said, reaching into the pocket of his jacket and coming out with an old corncob pipe. "I never knowed there was such bad blood 'tween 'em." He poked a forefinger into the pipe's bowl. Evidently satisfied with what he'd felt in there, he struck a match on the seat of his pants and fired the pipe up.

"Maybe they'll make up," Jessie said. She tried her best not to make a face as a breeze carried the aroma of Oakley's pipe tobacco her way. Whatever he was smoking, he'd paid too much for it. "Are you and Hank close friends?" she asked, coughing.

"Couldn't say close, but I'd be proud to call him a

friend," Oakley replied. "Hank's kind of a loner. He ain't too fond of joining in with the gang. I'll tell you one thing, though—"

He turned away from Jessie in order to spit a mouthful of tobacco juice into the dirt. Jessie made a bet with herself. Sure enough, when he looked back, globules of brown liquid were clinging to his beard.

"Tell you one thing, though, I wish they *would* bury the hatchet, ma'am. Hank Stills is a better lawman then all of us put together, and that includes Marshal Forbes, though he'd have my hide if he heard me say it. I feel like a fool being called the head deputy, when there's a man like Hank around."

Jessie was beginning to warm to the bearded deputy. He may have been a slob, but he was a good-hearted slob. "Well, I'm sure that Hank really does wish you well in your new job," she smiled, silently adding to herself, *Not that you're going to have it for more than a few minutes.*

"That's 'cause Hank's a gentleman," Oakley declared, puffing on his pipe. "Shame the marshal has told him to clear out of town—"

Two shots rang out in quick succession. "That last one came from inside the house!" Jessie exclaimed.

Oakley was already dashing up the flagstone path. He drew a Colt Peacemaker out of the flapped holster as he pushed open the front door. Jessie was right behind him, her own Colt in her hand.

The landlady was standing in the parlor. She was a buxom, gray-haired woman dressed in a faded pink flannel housecoat. She pointed to the staircase. "It came from up there!" she exclaimed. "But the only boarder home is Deputy Stills. He's got Marshal Forbes visiting—"

"The marshal?" Oakley asked, perplexed, as he began taking the stairs two at a time. "What's he doing here?"

Jessie started to follow.

"Ladies aren't allowed upstairs—" the landlady protested, but the look on Jessie's face, and the gun in her hand, made the woman think better of it.

By the time Jessie reached the top floor, Oakley was braced in the doorway of Stills's room. The bearded deputy was gripping his Peacemaker in both hands and pointing it at Stills. "Drop your pistol, Hank!" he ordered.

Jessie slipped past Oakley and into the room. Marshal Forbes was lying on the carpet. He was unconscious, and there was blood darkening the front of his tan shirt. The room's window was shattered. Glistening shards of glass were everywhere. Stills had his pistol in his hand, and smoke was curling out of its barrel.

"Drop your gun, I said," Oakley demanded. He was shaking, and his teeth were clenched so hard on the stem of his pipe that Jessie thought he was going to bite clear through it. "I'm arresting you for the murder of Marshal Forbes!"

"He ain't dead, Oakley," Stills said as he peered through the broken window. "And I didn't shoot him. The shot came from that rooftop across the way. I got a peek at who it was scrabbling across the shingles. It was that two-gun fella I tangled with earlier. I pegged a shot at him, but I missed—"

Oakley cut him off. "Please drop your gun!" he begged. "I don't want to shoot you, Hank!"

Jessie had managed to loosen Forbes's shoulder holster and tear away his blood-sodden shirt. "He's hurt bad, but he *is* still alive. The bullet hit him in the ribs on his right side."

"Listen to me, Oakley," Stills began patiently, as if he were speaking to a child. "You see that the window is busted—"

"Drop your gun!"

"—and you heard two shots. Who fired the second shot?"

"Two?" Oakley looked dazed, but only for a moment. "None of your tricks now, " he warned Stills. "All you've done is convince me that it wasn't self-defense. It's all as plain as day. You *lured* the marshal up here! Hank, I knowed that you two was at odds, but I never thought you'd shoot a man down like this!"

A rotund little fellow, dressed in a blue pinstriped suit and carrying a black satchel, shouldered his way past Oakley. He was the doctor, apparently summoned by the landlady.

Jessie got out of his way. "He's got some broken ribs," she began, "and maybe a punctured lung—"

"You looking to split the fee, miss?" the doctor scowled.

Jessie made a face and moved over to sit on Stills's narrow bed. The doctor was about forty, with thick, steel-rimmed spectacles and a full head of curly red hair. Jessie watched him take gauze and a bottle of carbolic acid solution out of his black bag and begin to swab the marshal's wound.

"Doesn't look too bad, Hank," the doctor told Stills. "But before I move him, I want to get the bullet out. I'll do it right here."

"You want Mrs. Donahue to lend a hand?" Stills asked.

"I wouldn't mind a slice of her apple pie, and some coffee," the doctor mused as he dunked a pair of forceps into the carbolic.

"Why the hell won't anybody listen to me?" Oakley complained. "I'm the head deputy!" he yelled. "While the marshal's hurt, I'm in charge!"

"Then do your job!" Stills roared so abruptly that it made Oakley flinch. "That gunslick is getting away right now!" He pointed his Colt out the window.

Oakley, his eyes glued to Stills's .44, lowered his own Peacemaker. "Why would one of Mr. Schiff's men shoot the marshal?" he demanded.

"'Cause he was aiming at *me,* is why!" Stills gritted his teeth, trying his best to keep calm. "I lit the lamp so that Cal could read—" He broke off abruptly.

Jessie, watching him, knew that Stills didn't want to reveal the evidence they'd found to Oakley. The man might take it upon himself either to confront or warn Schiff.

"Cal just got in the way of a bullet meant for me, is all," Stills weakly concluded.

"You're slick, Hank!" Oakley spat, shaking his head, "But I got you dead to rights! You have a motive for shooting the marshal, and I'm arresting you for it." He brought up his pistol. "For the last time, drop that there .44 or I'll shoot!"

"Hey, now," the doctor said softly, looking up from his patient. "Calm down, you two. No more shooting tonight. You boys see that I've got my hands full with Cal here. Hank, maybe you ought to go along with Oakley, just until Cal can straighten this out."

Stills gazed at the bearded deputy for a moment, then wearily nodded. He set his Colt down on the carpet and raised his hands. "We've known each other for a while, Oak. It's best we not let this get out of hand. You've arrested me, and now I'll come along quietly."

Oakley sagged with relief. "Thanks, Hank." He reached into his jacket pocket and tossed a set of handcuffs to Stills. "Would you mind?"

"That's not necessary!" Jessie said hotly.

"Stay out of this, ma'am," Oakley warned.

"Police business," Stills winked at her. He snapped the cuffs on himself. "Oakley, let me give you a piece of friendly advice," he drawled. "Next time you throw down on a man with a Peacemaker, take the time to cock the hammer. You're supposed to do that with a single-action gun."

"Shit, Hank," Oakley sighed tiredly. "I knowed that." He bent to pick up Stills's .44. "It's just that I was so shaky, I was afraid that if I hammered back, I might accidentally jerk on the trigger and shoot someone..." The bearded deputy's black eyes suddenly filled with tears. "You of all people, Hank," he began plaintively. "Why'd you have to do this?"

"Easy now," Stills soothed. "We'll get this straightened out, I promise. Doc, keep Cal healthy. The marshal's got to wake up if he's gonna clear me."

"Sorry, Hank. Cal's going to stay asleep for a while." The doctor probed at the wound with his forceps. "After I get the lead out of him and tape up his ribs, I'm going to give him some laudanum to keep him quiet. He'll be out through tomorrow, I'd wager."

"Damn," Stills muttered as Oakley began to lead him out of the room. "That leaves me stuck in jail!" He looked at Jessie and shrugged his shoulders. "Reckon you're gonna have to take that little ride we talked about all by your lonesome!"

★

Chapter 11

Jessie let Oakley lead his captive out of the boarding house before she left herself. The doctor was too engrossed in his surgery upon the marshal to notice her departure, and all Mrs. Donahue deigned to do was cluck disapprovingly as Jessie hurried out of the rooming house.

She did not head back toward Main Street, but cut through several back alleys toward the stables where her rented horse was being kept. With both Marshal Forbes and Deputy Stills out of action, Jessie was right back where she started. If she waited for Forbes to regain consciousness and clear Stills, Schiff and his men would have a day's head start in the search for Daniel Tang. She knew that the cattleman was counting on his rustlers to have already come across the boy. That was why Tang had volunteered to search Skinny Creek. Ki had tracked the rustlers there. If the boy was to have any chance at all of surviving, Jessie had to get to him first.

There were no lanterns to illuminate the back streets she was hurrying down. There was no one else around. Everybody not tucked into their homes had gathered at the marshal's office to gossip about the shooting. Jessie guessed that the saloons would do a good business later on tonight as men bought rounds and wagered on whether or not Stills did it.

Jessie worried about the contract she had given the deputy. It was the only thing that linked Schiff to his crimes. For a moment she wished that she had not turned the document over to Stills, but then she realized that their precious evidence could be in no safer place than tucked into the deputy's boot. In jail they took away a man's gun and belt, but not his boots. Oakley would not find the contract, and Stills himself was quite safe in jail. If anything should happen to her, the deputy could use the contract to muster up support for a posse to come rescue her, or avenge her death.

Such dismal thoughts in this dark and deserted section of town brought Jessie's mind around to Ki. She'd left her friend with Hiram Tang. Now that Tang was dead, buried by his son, who was also missing, it was not that farfetched to imagine that the samurai and the boy were together. If Ki was all right, he would have managed to contact her by now. All the more reason for her to waste no time in beginning her search for the two.

She turned a corner. Ahead of her was a long, narrow street. Warehouses on either side formed a manmade canyon. The street was a gauntlet of shadows Jessie had to travel before she could reach the relative shelter of the stable.

Jessie gave herself a good scolding for being afraid of the dark at a time like this! And yet, as she began to stride down the street, her hand unaccountably found its way to the butt of her Colt. Something was making her nervous. She wished she had Ki by her side...

Jessie froze in midstep. Had she imagined it, or had she heard the footfall of someone behind her? She resisted the impulse to turn around. If someone was following her, it would not help matters to let him know that she'd heard him.

She walked on. Ki was not here, but she did have the benefit of all he had taught her. She heard no more footsteps, but that did not mean she hadn't heard that first one! Ki would have scoffed that it was typically Western to ignore one's instincts in favor of one's so-called rationality. Now, instead of scolding herself for her nervousness, she quieted her skepticism in order to give her agitation free rein.

"The body knows," Ki had once told her. *"The body will account for itself if only the mind will let it."* To prove his point, Ki had used the example of the archer who hits his target only when he gives up his anxiousness about accuracy. Jessie herself had practiced target shooting from her quick-draw stance, and had realized that if she wanted to hit anything by firing so quickly from the hip, she had to let her reflexes take over—it all happened too fast for her to consciously *try* to take aim.

But that had been for practice. The situation she was in now was for real. Jessie discovered that she had instinctively moved out into the center of the dark street. The stable ahead was growing ever closer. As Jessie walked on as silently as she could, she tried to focus her hearing behind her, imagining—as Ki had taught her to imagine—that she had *fingers* of hearing that could reach back to detect the presence of her adversary.

Jessie now had no doubt that someone was following her. Her fear-charged instincts had overcome the meek protests of her rational mind.

Whoever was tailing her was hanging back. He'd obviously figured out that she was heading for the stable, and was waiting to make his move inside its confines.

Jessie reached the old wooden double doors of the stable and hauled them open, their rusty hinges squeaking like the rats that were even now skittering to their holes as Jessie entered. She'd hoped that the stableboy would be around, but she had no such luck. She would be all alone as she saddled her tan gelding and waited for her tail to make his play.

In the stalls, the horses bobbed their heads nervously as

Jessie struck a match and used it to light a stub of candle stuck in a glob of candlewax on the rack where the saddles were hung to air out. Jessie soothed her own horse and then left his stall in order to lug over her saddle and bridle. She placed her gear on top of two stacked bales of hay, and led her mount out of its stall. She had no wish to be trapped in the narrow stall by whoever was now lurking outside the stable.

First she bridled her horse, looping its reins around the handle of a pitchfork stuck into a hay bale, knowing that the animal was well trained and wouldn't bolt, even though the reins weren't tied securely. Then she wrestled the heavy, double-rigged saddle, with its two cinches and high steel horn, across his back.

Jessie was just finishing tightening the second of the two cinches when the stable doors were pulled open. She whirled around, but her night vision had been spoiled by the candlelight. She peered and squinted into the darkness, seeing nothing, until she remembered what Ki had taught her, and turned her gaze aside to look in the direction of the noise out of the corners of her eyes.

Now she could make out the silhoutte of a man framed in the doorway. There was no doubt about his identity as he swept back his coat flaps to reveal the jutting grips of a brace of pistols strapped around his waist.

"Stay where you are," Jessie warned as the man entered the stables, "or I'll mess you up worse than Deputy Stills did."

Schiff's gunslick kept coming. Briefly, Jessie considered dropping the man where he stood. It was an easy enough shot, and she knew she had the advantage of surprise. It had been her experience that few men took a woman who wore a gun seriously. She began to draw her Colt, but hesitated and then gave the idea up. For one thing, Deputy Stills had said that this fellow was the one who had shot Marshal Forbes. If that was so, he might be needed alive to clear Stills if Forbes—despite the doctor's assurances—should take a turn for the worse. For another thing, even though Jessie knew the man confronting her was up to no good, she could not throw down on him until he attacked.

"Now, them ain't Texas manners, young lady," the man said, mumbling oddly. "That ain't how you treated Deputy Stills when he came calling."

Jessie gasped as the gunslick came into the circle of light cast by the candle. His mouth and nose were badly torn. Evidently the fall he'd taken at Stills's hands had caused more damage than Jessie had realized. Pinpoints of blood dotted the less lacerated areas of the man's face. The injuries would take long, painful weeks to heal, weeks in which them man would be tortured by every bite of food and drop of liquid he took. And even when the healing process was over, there were sure to be disfiguring scars.

"Whatsamatter?" the gunslick growled through his mangled lips. He spat a mouthful of blood. "Doncha like how I look? You was there when it happened. Hell, it happened on account of you!"

"Mister, you ought to be looking for a doctor, not another fight," Jessie said. "You've got to get the dirt out of those cuts."

"Tried to wash 'em out with whiskey," the man whined. "Hurts too much!" His dirty fingers daubed at his wounds in frustration, like an animal gnawing at its own limb caught in a trap. "Damn that deputy for doing this to me!" he snarled.

"Is that why you tried to ambush him in his room?" Jessie demanded. Seeing his surprise, she added, "Stills told me that he saw you." As she spoke, she glanced past the gunslick. She could see the street through the stable's opened doors. The entire length of that dark avenue was deserted. She stared into the man's eyes. They were glazed with pain and glaring like a rattler's black eyes just before it strikes. She was all alone with a killer whose pain was goading him into a state bordering on insanity.

"Shot at Stills on my own," the gunslick lisped in reply. "Schiff don't know nothin' about it." He spat more blood, and moaned. "Would've gotten him, too, but Forbes crossed into the bullet." Rivulets of blood dripped from his teeth as he grinned, but his merriment passed quickly as he groaned, "Oh, my mouth! I like the way it turned out though. Don't matter what *you* believe. Stills is framed nice and neat by my murdering Forbes."

Jessie was about to correct him, but then thought better of it. Let him think that Forbes was dead, that way he wouldn't be tempted to make another try at Stills.

"Be right fine to see that bastard deputy strung up for my crime," the gunslick said. "Can't wait to see it."

"What do you want with me?" Jessie asked. "I've done you no harm—"

"No harm!" the gunslick interrupted, laughing giddily. "Look at me!" he gestured toward his maimed face and tattered clothes. "This happened to me on account of you!"

"You'll heal—"

"But my lips is split so that I'll talk funny. And my nose is busted. I'll have these scars forever, and everywhere I go they'll tell the story 'bout how I got bested," he moaned. "They'll see my face and know that them stories is true!" He reached inside his coat pocket, coming out with a folding knife. He pried the three-inch blade open, and waved it menacingly in front of Jessie. "I'm going to cut you so that you look worse than me," he vowed, advancing upon her. "I'm going to carve—"

There was no time for Jessie to draw her Colt. She went into the relaxed, supple stance Ki had taught her, balanced on the balls of her feet. The *jujutsu* stance.

As the gunslick jabbed his blade toward her face, Jessie brought up her hands, locking her fingers about his wrist. She did not try to deflect his lunge, but instead added her own strength to his powerful thrust. When Ki had taught Jessie the rudiments of this unarmed combat technique, he had explained that the Chinese character *ju* meant "submissive and pliable." One did not confront an enemy's strength, but blended into it, and then controlled it.

It took only the slightest exertion on Jessie's part to change the blade's direction so that it stabbed nothing but the empty air above her shoulder. *Jujutsu* did not demand the long years of practice that led to the steely muscles and mental discipline required of *te,* Ki's favored method of unarmed combat. What did demand was "the flexibility of the pine bough beneath the weight of snow."

The gunslick's body followed the trajectory set by his jabbing arm. He had put his shoulder into the thrust, and now he began to topple in that direction, caught totally off balance. Jessie spun around so that her back was against his chest, and then she wedged her own shoulder into his armpit. Then she bent, like that pine branch beneath the load of snow, jackknifing her body at the waist and pulling down on the gunslick's extended arm. It was his own weight and force that sent his feet flying over his head. He flipped over Jessie to slam his spine hard against the packed-earth floor of the stable. Jessie went for her Colt.

The knife went flying, but the man was incredibly fast. He'd managed to flip over onto his belly and snatch at Jessie's boots, pulling her feet out from under her before her pistol could clear leather. She fell back against the hay bales. Her gun fell out of reach as the pitchfork toppled handle-first toward the floor. Her horse, its reins free, danced away from the scuffle.

The gunslick was clawing his way up Jessie's legs. She grasped the handle of the pitchfork and jammed the tip of the handle into the gunslick's face.

The pole struck only a light and glancing blow, but the man's face was already so sensitive that he screamed in agony and rolled away. He was on his back, drawing his gun with his right hand, as Jessie rose up on her knees, the pitchfork still in her grip. She reversed it and stabbed down at the slick's gun. His wrist was caught between the fork's tines and pinned to the earthen floor. He spent a precious second trying to wriggle his right hand free as Jessie dove for her gun. His left hand was just clearing his second gun from its holster when Jessie snatched up her own Colt, flipped over onto her back, and fired across her own chest. Her bullets stitched their way up his side. She'd hit him twice, but evidently not anywhere vital, for he was bringing his own gun to bear upon her. She fired twice more, as fast as her Colt's mechanism could respond to her trigger finger. To Jessie it was like a nightmare. She and the man were both horizontal, separated by inches. Jessie's own Colt was so close to her face that she could feel burning powder stinging her cheeks. Each time she fired, blue lightning licked out of her gun barrel to overpower the flickering light of the candle. The muzzle flashes seared a scorchmark across the silk of her blouse. Delicate curls of smoke rose from around the edges of the bullet holes she was punching into the man's jacket. Each time his gun rose, one of Jessie's rounds forced it back down.

Jessie fired once more, and then her Colt clicked empty. It had taken her no more than a moment to squeeze off the entire cylinder. The five separate explosions had sounded to her like one single, continuous blast of gunfire. In the rush of silence, she became aware of the horses' screams, and the dull thuds as they kicked at their stalls.

Her assailant's pistol seemed trained right at her head. Jessie stared into the black hole of its muzzle and waited for the gunslick to take his turn.

Suddenly a panicked rat careened madly from out of some dark corner. The rat skittered across the man's chest. Jessie was so keyed up that she automatically tracked the rodent with her pistol. Her Colt clicked empty three more times before she could stop herself.

The rat disappeared back into the shadows. The would-be killer had not moved.

Jessie rose up to a kneeling position to stare into his open, sightless eyes.

She wondered when it was that he had died. She'd been too busy pumping lead into him to notice.

She climbed to her feet, jamming her Colt into its holster. Her mount was in the far corner of the stable. She approached it slowly, speaking in low, soft tones, until it was calm enough to be touched. Then she began to lead it toward the stable doors, pausing only to blow out the candle.

Once outside, Jessie mounted quickly and rode off at a gallop down the alley through which she'd come. She could hear shouts and see lights winking on in windows all over this end of town as she heeled the tan gelding out of Nettle Grove.

After she'd left the last of the town's buildings far behind her, she breathed deeply of the cool night air. She was glad to be alive, and now she thought once again about Ki and young Danny Tang. She gave her horse its head, and rode like hell for Skinny Creek.

★

Chapter 12

Dawn's first light was a thin gray line to the east as Jessie reached the bend in the trail just before Skinny Creek. During her hard ride, she'd passed the granite outcropping where she, Ki, and Hiram Tang had made their stand against the rustlers. The rocks were mere inkblots in the darkness when she passed them, and that had been just as well, for she'd left Ki among those boulders, and she had no desire to know if any of them were stained with his blood.

She slowed her sweat-lathered gelding to a walk in order to cool it down as she reached the town's outskirts. Now that she was here, she wondered what her next move should be. Skinny Creek didn't look like it was loaded with options; the one narrow street, sporadically studded with ramshackle buildings, looked like a ghost town.

Only one building in the entire town had light shining from its windows. Jessie figured that whoever was in there was probably awake, and that the only awake person in Skinny Creek was probably her best starting place.

The building was the general store. Jessie wrapped her

horse's reins around the hitch rail outside the brightly lit windows, thinking it was odd that a store would be open at this ungodly hour. Jessie peeked in. She saw a pretty, black-haired woman dressed in a calico skirt and blue work shirt. A bandolier of shotgun shells was loosely draped across her chest. The woman was laboriously coiling a great length of manila rope. On the counter beside her were several canteens and a small rucksack.

As Jessie entered the store, the woman spun around, glaring suspiciously. "Hello—" was all Jessie managed to get out. The woman snatched up a sawed-off, double-barreled shotgun from its place of concealment behind the rucksack, and leveled it at her.

Jessie crabbed sideways, drawing her own Colt and thanking her lucky stars that she'd taken the time to reload during her ride. Her eyes desperately scanned the store, but there was no place to take cover.

"Just you hold it right there!" the woman storekeeper demanded.

Jessie racked her brains for an appropriate comeback, but all she could think of was, "You hold it too!" It sounded woefully inadequate for the occasion, about as inadequate as her own .38-caliber revolver in a toe-to-toe tussle against a double-barreled twelve-gauge.

"Who are you and what do you want?" the woman asked.

"My name is Jessica Starbuck. I'm looking for a man and a boy. They're my friends and I'm worried about them."

"Ki and Danny?" the woman asked.

Jessie felt like crying, her relief was so great. The other woman evidently saw it in Jessie's face, for her own features softened. She lowered her shotgun.

"You know where they are?" Jessie begged. She put away her Colt. "Is Ki all right?"

"He's . . . well," the woman replied, her voice breaking slightly. "The boy is fine." She stuck out her hand. "My name's Mary Hudson."

Jessie shook her hand. "Mary, where are they? Are they here?" she asked hopefully.

"No," the woman said sadly. "What I wouldn't *give* to have that man and that boy here with me. They're being held prisoner by a band of outlaws."

"The rustlers!" Jessie cut in. "Ki had been searching for their hideout. Mary, do you know where it is?"

"I do," she said proudly. "They're hiding out in the abandoned silver mine."

"How many of them are there?"

"Seven. But they're splitting up," Mary said excitedly. "A bunch of 'em will be riding out at dawn to let their boss know that they've got the boy. I don't know who the boss is," she added as an afterthought.

"I do," Jessie said. "And so does the law in Nettle Grove. They'll be coming to back us up, but we can't wait for them. We've got to free Ki and Daniel before the rustlers get orders to kill them."

Mary looked Jessie up and down, taking her measure. "There's nobody we can turn to for help help here in Skinny Creek," she warned. "If any rescuing is going to be done, it's up to us to do it." Her pale blue eyes narrowed. "Are you game for a fight, maybe to the death?"

Jessie suddenly understood the significance of the rucksack, canteens, rope, and bandolier of shotgun shells. "You were getting ready to try and mount a rescue all by your self, weren't you?"

"Yep."

"But why?"

"I lost my family a while ago," Mary began, shouldering her rucksack. "That's all finished with, but I don't aim to see another fine pair of menfolk pass to dust before their rightful times. Lost a pair, and now I'm going to save a pair, or die trying," she said defiantly. "Are you with me?" The sparkle in Jessie's green eyes, and her grin, stopped her. "Well, I'll be a horse's ass," Mary said softly. "You came here all by yourself to rescue them, didn't you?"

"Ki has saved my life many times," Jessie replied. "I hope I'll be able to repay the favor this morning."

"Just what is he to you?" Mary asked. "I mean, Ki told

me that the boy is an orphan, and that he himself has friends. Just what kind of friend are you?"

Jessie shouldered the heavy coil of rope and the canteens. "Why don't we talk on the way? How are we going to do this? We can't just sashay in and ask the rustlers to hand them over. If they're in a mine, that means there's only one entrance—"

"That's what everybody thinks," Mary smiled, taking up her shotgun and heading for the door. "But I know another way in."

Jessie left her horse where it was. Mary explained that it was only a half-mile trek to the back of the hill into which the mine had been dug. Once there, the grade they'd have to climb would be too steep for horses. They made most of the walk in silence, listening to their boots squeak against the dry earth and prickly grass, and watching the crack-willows take shape in the slowly gathering light. Once, Mary motioned for Jessie to crouch down behind some sandstone boulders as a group of riders passed by in the distance.

"Those will be the boys riding to tell their boss what they've got," Mary said. She squinted and stared at the cloud of dust the riders were raising. "Hard to see in this half-light, but I counted three."

"So did I," Jessie replied. "That means there's four of them in the mine. This is starting to feel better and better to me," she said confidently. "We're armed, and we'll have the advantage of surprise. We might even catch those four cow thieves napping. And if we can cut Ki loose, he'll be able to dispose of the four all by himself."

Mary looked sideways at Jessie, but said nothing.

"You said Ki was all right?"

"It'll be sunrise in half an hour," Mary remarked. "Let's go."

The hill they had to climb rose up before them. Jessie stood at its base and craned her neck to see the top. "We can't walk this," she began, shaking her head.

"This side is steeper than the front," Mary admitted. "You don't sound too happy. You afraid?"

"Not being happy isn't the same thing as being afraid," Jessie said dourly. "After you."

They started by walking, but soon were reduced to moving up on all fours. Several times the rocks and loose earth gave way, sending them skidding down on their bellies. They scrabbled for handholds, and soon their fingers were cut and bleeding. Mary unwound a length of rope and tied one end around her waist, instructing Jessie to do the same. Linked together, the two women took turns taking the lead and hauling each other up.

"How much more?" Jessie huffed. Her clothing and skin were coated with dust, and her copper-gold tresses hung in damp ringlets around her face. She unscrewed the top of one of the canteens and rinsed her mouth clean of the alkaline film that coated it. Then she took a long drink and handed the canteen to Mary.

"We're almost there," Mary promised. She spat out a mouthful of water and watched the dry earth suck it in.

"I'll tell you one thing," Jessie said. "If we're going to make it and be in condition to do something other than surrender, we're going to have to leave most of this gear behind. Take your shotgun and shells and one of these canteens. I'll take another, and the rope." She pointed to the rucksack on Mary's back. "What's in there, anyway?"

Mary shrugged. "A couple of knives, candles, bandages, whiskey . . ."

Jessie shook her head, laughing. "Just like a couple of women to overpack for such a short trip."

Mary, laughing also, dropped her sack. She slipped the short length of her shotgun through her bandolier. She reached out to give Jessie a hand, and together they resumed climbing.

A few minutes later Mary said, "You never did tell me what Ki is to you."

"Listen, I like girl-talk as much as the next female,"

Jessie groaned, "but can't it wait until we take our next rest? I really don't think I can talk and climb at the same time."

"Well, you don't have to climb anymore," Mary chuckled. "We're here." She pointed to a cavelike opening about five feet wide just a few yards higher, and to their left. Boulders framed this back entrance to the mine. "It's a natural passageway," Mary explained. "When the mine was active, one of the main tunnels branched off into a drift that connected with this opening. The rustlers just use the main cavern. They'd have had no reason to explore the rear of the mine, so they can't know about this entrance."

"Well, let's take a few moments to catch our breath and then go on in," Jessie said as they settled themselves at the mouth of the opening. "To answer your question about Ki and myself, we grew up together on my father's ranch. You might say that he works for me, but we're much more like sister and brother than employer and employee."

"Sister and brother," Mary slowly repeated. "Do you mean—"

"I mean exactly that," Jessie softly reassured her. "You've gotten kind of sweet on him, haven't you?"

"Reckon I have," Mary admitted. "I can't get him and that young orphan boy out of mind. Oh, I know that Ki ain't the settling-down kind, but now that he's—" She stopped abruptly.

"What were you going to say?"

"Look, the sun's coming up behind those hills! We've got to hurry!" She jumped to her feet, tugging on the rope tied around Jessie's waist.

For a moment Jessie thought the woman was just trying to change the subject, but the fear in Mary Hudson's eyes convinced her that her plea was genuine. "What's so important about sunrise? It's always going to be dark inside the mine."

"We've got to get through the tunnel *before* daylight."

"Lord," she fretted, "I'm afraid I misjudged the time.

We haven't a second to spare!" She disappeared into the darkness of the cave.

Jessie followed. After a few steps in, the dim light coming through the entranceway faded. They were in a blackness so dense that Jessie could not see, but only feel the taut rope pulling her forward. Several times she stumbled, but Mary urged her on.

"Feel your way along the wall," she whispered. "There's wind from the outside pushing at our backs. We can't get lost, but we've got to hurry."

"I still don't see why—" Jessie started to say, but her mouth shut against a scream as something furry brushed past her ear. "Mary, what was that?" she gasped, hearing the storekeeper's yelp of fear as the flying thing passed her. Jessie felt a thud against her sweat-damp back, and then a fluttering, bouncing force against her spine. It was mothlike, but much too large and heavy to be an insect. The creature clambered up her back, perched on her shoulder for an instant, and then took off. As it did, its dry, leathery wing scraped Jessie's cheek. "Mary!" she screamed, and then gagged as a horrible stench filled nostrils. Her boots began to slip against something wet and slimy.

"Bats!" the woman ahead of her hissed. "We're in their nesting cavern right now. They've been out feeding all night, and now that's it's day, they'll be coming home to roost! These few right now are just the first! If we don't get past this cavern quickly, the whole swarm of them will be on top of us!"

"Listen!" Jessie whispered as they hurried on, their hands brushing the walls of the narrow passageway. "I can hear them!"

At first the squeaks were faint, but they grew in volume even as Jessie spoke. She looked behind her, but was able to see nothing through the velvety blackness except the small patch of light that was the cave's now-distant entrance. As she stared, the pale circle of light suddenly winked out, and then began to twinkle as hundreds of flapping shapes swooped through. "They've entered the cave!" she shouted. "They're right behind us! Run!"

They stumbled on, hearing the ever-increasing squeaking, and imagining the flood of bats cascading their way like a torrent of water along a pipe. *They won't bite, they won't bite,* Jessie told herself. *They eat bugs, they eat fruit, not flesh—*

But what if they think we're attacking nests? Jessie wondered in panic. *What if—*

The beginnings of the swarm broke like a wave against their backs. The bats squeaked in fear and panic. They twisted and dove in an attempt to avoid colliding with Jessie and Mary, but the passage was just too narrow.

Jessie pulled her Stetson's brim down as low as it could go, and wrapped her arms about her head to protect her face. She stumbled on, along with and right through what was now a solid storm of hot, pulsing, furry bodies and madly beating, leathery wings. The vermins' smell was suffocating, and their screeching filled her ears. She thought of Mary, who had no hat. She could hear the woman's mewls of terror as they both pushed forward.

"I—I can't!" Mary whimpered. "I—"

Jessie felt the rope go slack as Mary slumped down to the cavern's floor. She shuffled forward, hands extended.

"Oh, God!" Mary suddenly screamed. "They're landing on me!"

Jessie literally tripped over the cowering woman. Mary was covered with bats. The creatures, confused by the noise she and Mary had been making, could not find their way to their true perches. Since Jessie was still moving, they did not land on her, but Mary, huddled on the floor, was a relatively still object to the creatures, whose instincts told them that it was time to roost.

Jessie climbed past Mary, and then turned to brush the bats off her. As she did so, Jessie's hands came upon the stock of the woman's sawed-off shotgun. She pulled it free of Mary's bandolier.

"W-what are you going to do?" Mary asked, trembling.

"Just keep your head down, and move fast when I tell you," Jessie commanded. She back-pedaled the length of the rope connecting her to Mary, cocked both hammers of the shotgun, and let fly.

The double *BOOM!* within the close confines of the passageway was earsplitting. For a split second the darkness turned to brilliant blue, revealing a vision out of hell. The main part of the swarm was still hovering behind them. The bats flitted against the walls of the tunnel, unable to get through. Jessie saw a solid layer of the bats torn into bloody bits by the fast-spreading shot pattern that erupted from the short-barreled gun. The rest of the bats—their sensitive eyes blinded by the muzzle flash, their finely-honed sense of hearing disrupted by the noise of the explosion—began to swoop crazily, dashing themselves against the ceiling, floor, and walls of the cavern. Their wings made a sound like paper being crumpled. Jessie heard the light thudding of their bodies falling to the floor as she pulled at the rope, reeling Mary in.

"Let's go!" Jessie shouted, too loudly, for the blast was still ringing in her own ears, just as her eyes were still stained with the afterimage of the shotgun's flash. *Let's go,* she thought. *But which way?* She'd gotten herself turned around several times, and was no longer sure which way was forward, and which was back the way they'd come.

Mary sensed her indecision, and said, "Feel the air current? Let the wind push us along!"

Arms linked, they ran on. Ahead of them, wavering amber lanternlight shone from a side passage. Jessie reached it first, and pulled Mary through.

The two women had no time to react as strong arms locked around their throats. The shotgun was torn from Jessie's fingers and her Colt was plucked from its holster. Then Jessie was sent sprawling. Mary landed beside her.

Two rustlers stood over them and laughed. "We heard you coming a mile away," one said. "Noise travels pretty good through these caves." He picked up a Winchester that had been leaning against the wall and leveled it at the women.

"We didn't know there was another way in here," his partner explained as he gathered up Mary's shotgun. "When we heard your screams, we came explorin'." He jammed Jessie's Colt into his gunbelt, and then picked up the kerosene lantern the two men had brought with them. "Follow me," he ordered.

Jessie and Mary slowly got to their feet. They brushed themselves off and began to trudge along behind the rustler. His partner brought up the rear. "Keep it nice and slow," he growled, prodding them along with the barrel of his Winchester.

"You're going to be sorry for this," Mary threatened.

"You're the one who'll be sorry, Mary," the rifleman spat.

"How does he know your name?" Jessie asked Mary.

"These cow thieves have been stealing goods from me just like they've been taking what they've wanted from others in Skinny Creek. They strut through the town like they own it. 'Course when a *real* man, like Ki, comes looking for them, they hide in this stinking cave. Just like those damned bats," she added contemptuously.

"Now it's the chink who's blind as a bat," the rifleman snorted.

"What?" Jessie broke in. "Mary, what's he talking about?" she asked anxiously.

"You didn't know your boyfriend was blinded?" the rifleman laughed.

"I'm sorry, Jessie," Mary murmured softly. "Ki was injured. A bullet grazed his head. He lost his sight. I was going to tell you—Jessie!"

Mary caught her up as Jessie's knees buckled and she began to slump to the floor of the cave. "One of you men help me!" the storekeeper demanded.

"This some kind of trick?" the man holding the lantern asked suspiciously.

“No!” Mary said impatiently. “Help me with her! Can’t you see how pale she is? She’s fainting.”

“All right. Mike, you carry her,” the rifleman ordered, taking charge. “I’ll carry the lantern.” He prodded Mary’s spine with his Winchester. “Don’t make it worse for yourself, Mary,” he growled. “Tim will decide what’s going to happen to you two females along with the chink and the kid, as soon as he gets back. All we’re going to do now is tie you up.”

Jessie, meanwhile, shrank away from the grumbling rustler’s enfolding arms. “I’m all right,” she mumbled. “I can walk on my own.” She wiped away the tears that had suddenly flooded her eyes. “I just want to see Ki.”

“That’s where we’re taking you,” the rifleman replied. “Get moving.”

★

Chapter 13

Jessie and Mary were herded into the main chamber of the abandoned mine. The two rustlers who had stayed behind to guard Ki and Danny were sharing a meal of beef jerky and whiskey. Their rifles were close beside them.

"Everything go okay?" they asked as the two rustlers who had caught Jessie and Mary proudly displayed their captives.

"Ran right into our arms," the rifleman snorted. "Let's go, you two." He led them past several stacks of crated supplies, over to the flour sacks upon which Ki and Danny were glumly resting.

"Hey," Danny whispered to Ki. "Mary is back, and there's Miss Starbuck!"

Ki sat up quickly, swiveling his head in the direction of the approaching footsteps. "Jessie?"

"Oh, Ki, is it true?" Jessie gasped. She tried to run to him, but the rustler barred her way with his Winchester.

"You all can have a nice little chat in just a minute," he

laughed. "But first . . ." He relieved Mary of her cartridge bandolier, and Jessie of her coil of rope. He cut two short lengths from the latter, and bound both women's hands tightly in front. "You two sit down right beside the chink, and keep it quiet, or we'll be back to gag you." With that, he retreated to join his three buddies around their bottle.

"Ki," Jessie whispered, "can you see anything at all?" She peered into his face, at his staring eyes.

"Do not worry," Ki confided. "My vision is slowly returning." He frowned. "Too slowly to do us any good in this predicament, I fear. I can distinguish between light and darkness, but that's all."

Jessie brought up her bound hands to gently brush back his blue-black hair. "We'll get the finest doctors. You'll see, everything will be all right! Oh, Ki," she sighed. "I'm so glad you're alive."

"It's good to hear your voice," Ki replied thickly, and then, as if embarrassed by his show of emotion, he added gruffly, "But you were foolish to come here. The situation was bad enough when I had only Danny to look out for, but now, with three of you . . ."

"Miss Starbuck," Danny interrupted, "is anybody coming to help us?"

Jessie looked over her shoulder to make sure that the four rustlers were too far away to overhear. "We can expect help, but not for a while. It's up to us to get ourselves out of this."

A burst of laughter from the four rustlers distracted Jessie.

"Celebrating our capture," Mary said wryly.

"Actually, Danny has told me that they've been drinking heavily for quite some time," Ki remarked. "They have slept only fitfully. Soon they'll fall asleep. We will wait . . ."

"I'm pretty tired myself," Jessie yawned. "Can't remember when I slept last."

"Then sleep now," Ki suggested. "Danny and Mary, you both sleep as well. When the time comes for us to make our move, we'll need to be as fresh as possible."

"What are we going to do?" Mary asked. "Except for that little knife I brought you, we've got no weapons."

"That's not quite true," Jessie smiled.

"Indeed," Ki chuckled, smiling in Jessie's direction.

"What is this, a private joke?" Mary asked.

"Keep quiet!" one of the rustlers shouted at them. He rolled his eyes, muttering, "Women!" His three friends broke into drunken laughter.

"We've got to keep our voices down," Jessie whispered. "Mary, all I meant was that I've got a derringer tucked into my boot. But it's only got two shots, and I've no more cartridges in my pockets."

"There's four rustlers," Mary insisted stubbornly. "What are we going to do—"

"Exactly what I tell you to do," Ki cut in. "When the time comes, I will be the weapon, but all of you must be my eyes. Now sleep!"

Jessie moved to sit beside Danny. She slumped down, resting her head against one of the flour sacks. Now that she was with Ki, she felt safe and secure, even though they were prisoners. Her eyelids felt as heavy as lead. The gunfight in the stable and her long ride to Skinny Creek had exhausted her. Her ordeal in the cave had used up every last bit of her stamina. The flour sack felt as soft and comfortable as any feather bed. In just seconds she was sound asleep.

Danny rested his head against her soft, warm shoulder. Ever since his father's death the boy had been living through the days in a numb state that was close to shock. Sleep had been impossible. Every time he closed his eyes he saw his father lying in the shallow grave Danny had dug. Only Ki's calming, soothing presence had kept the boy's nerves from completely unraveling. The boy shut his eyes, meaning only to rest them for a moment.

Ki, hearing Danny's fidgeting and his irregular breathing, whispered, "I want you to sleep, Daniel . . ."

"I can't," the boy said, sobbing softly. "I keep thinking about my father."

"He would have been proud of you these last days." Ki said.

"Y-yeah?" Danny sniffled loudly, and wiped at his nose. "Y-you think so?"

"Of course. Did you not save my life?"

"I guess I did," the boy said, awestruck.

"Danny, are your eyes closed?" Ki asked.

"Yes."

"Good," the samurai said. "I want you to count your breaths. Think of nothing but counting your breaths. One, two, three . . ."

After a moment's silence, Danny asked drowsily, "Ki? What happens to orphans?"

The samurai paused before answering. "I haven't told you before, Danny, but I too am an orphan."

"Y-you?" Danny asked, amazed. "Could I be like you, then?"

"You already are," Ki said quietly but firmly. "Sleep, Danny."

The boy's breathing grew both deep and regular. Just before he slipped into unconsciousness he gave a gentle tug on the rope that ran from his bound wrists to Ki's. Then, as if reassured that the samurai would remain close by, Daniel finally slept.

"More than rope binds us together," Ki told the softly snoring boy.

"I think he's adopted you," Mary said. "Dan needs a father and a mother," she added meaningfully. "You and me being here with him, well, it seems kind'a *fated* to be . . ."

"I think this conversation is headed in a direction I do not wish to travel," Ki replied dryly. "Sleep, Mary."

"I'm not tired," she sulked. "But I *am* cold!" She sidled up against him. After a moment she asked, "Is your sight really coming back?"

"Yes."

"Great," she replied, in a noncommittal tone.

"Mary, what is bothering you?" Ki asked patiently.

"Well," she pouted, "I sorta thought that maybe you'd been thinking of staying with me. But now that you're getting better..."

"Mary," Ki began gently, "I am very fond of you, but—"

"Oh, hush," she said firmly. "No need to explain. Anyway, mister, a woman doesn't ever want to hear the reasons why a man *doesn't* want her." She sighed. "I wonder if there's a woman on earth who could rope you in."

"I'm sorry," Ki said tenderly.

"So am I," Mary shrugged. "Well, since we'll soon be saying goodbye"—she glanced over her shoulder toward the four rustlers—"one way or the other, I reckon I might as well take fun when I can get it. My wrists may be tied together, but my fingers are free." She reached into Ki's lap and began to unbutton the front of his denims.

"Mary, we are not alone," Ki reminded her. He tried to stop her, but she moved too fast for his blindly groping hands. "Danny and Jessie are right beside us!"

"So? I won't be the one to wake them up!" she smirked. "My husband and I used to make love with our son right beside us in our bed. When you live in a one-room cabin along with your child, you learn to take pleasure quietly, or not at all!"

"What about the guards?" Ki protested weakly. Despite himself, he felt his erection swelling as she tugged his pants down past his hips.

"Don't worry about them," Mary said. "They're all the way across the cavern, and there's stacks of crates between us and them. Two of them are already asleep, and the other pair is acting piss-drunk! Why, the whiskey has made them so forgetful that they're not even bothering to refill the kerosene lanterns. The flames are all flickering mighty low. We'll be in darkness in a little while."

"In that case," Ki chuckled. He twisted his wrists, and the coils of rope around them dropped away.

Mary gaped. "How'd you do that?"

"I have been working on the knots ever since they tied

my hands," he confided. "It occupied my mind while they kept me here."

"Why didn't you use the knife I sewed into your shirt?"

"The guards have been checking my bonds every now and then," Ki explained. "It was an easy matter to gather up the slack and pretend to still be tied, but the guards would have noticed a severed rope."

Mary's nimble fingers stroked him into full hardness. "Gee, I was kinda looking forward to having you with your hands tied," she simpered. "Oh, well, beggars can't be choosers!" With that, she hiked up her skirt and then forked one thigh across Ki, mounting him like a saddled pony. Sighing contentedly, she settled herself upon his lap.

Ki did his best to stifle his gasp of pleasure. She was so wet that he slid deep into her. He tightened his buttocks and thrust up to meet her as she twisted and bucked upon him. All the while she moaned faintly, like some distant wind sweeping across the plains.

Mary came almost immediately. Ki could not see her, but he could certainly feel the rhythmic contractions of her inner muscles. He ran his hands beneath her skirt, to caress her warm, velvet-smooth backside enticingly splayed across his groin. Mary began to slide up and down, so expertly that Ki had to bite down on his lower lip to keep from crying out as he gushed inside of her.

"There now," Mary whispered sweetly in his ear. "Wasn't that just *wonderful*?"

Ki had to admit that it was. The fact that there were other people in such close proximity seemed to add a spicy tang to their love-play. Mary evidently felt the same way, for she was far from being finished with him. She lifted herself off, to trail her long hair down his belly. Ki ran his hands across her lithe, muscular legs as she began to kiss and lick his flaccid shaft, soon bringing it back to attention.

Not being able to see what this female was going to do to him next only added to his enjoyment. Ki remembered that geishas often blindfolded their lords before beginning lovemaking. He himself had never tried the trick, but now he understood why it was so popular in Japan. Not being able to see definitely increased the intensity of physical sensation. Mary's swirling, twirling tongue upon his marble-hard erection was sending waves of shivering delight up and down his spine.

Ki tried to pull away, but Mary only hummed, "Uh-uh," and took a firm hold upon him. She was like a little girl licking a lollypop. As she devoured her treat, her bottom wagged and twitched against his chest like a happy puppy's tail.

Ki could hold back no longer. He stuffed a handful of her skirt into his mouth to muffle his long, hoarse moan of almost painful ecstasy.

Mary finally sat up. Ki could hear licking her lips. She reversed her position, and nestled her head against his chest. Sighing happily, she sank quickly into a deep, contented sleep.

Jessie stirred, and opened her eyes to see Ki crouched above her. His fingers stroked her hair, and then lightly glided down to trace the features of her face. As he reached her lips, he pressed his fingertips gently against them to keep her from talking.

"It has been several hours," he whispered. "Mary and the boy are still asleep. Do not wake them. The less noise, the better. I think it is time for us to attack, but I need you to look and tell me if the four guards are indeed asleep." He removed the *shuriken* throwing blade Mary had sewn into his shirt, and quickly sliced away the rope binding Jessie's hands.

Jessie sat up. She craned her neck to peer over the stacked crates. "Yes," she whispered. "Three of them are sleeping, and the fourth is just barely awake. He's got a rifle across his lap, but his head is nodding."

"All right," Ki said in satisfaction. "I will kill him now."

"But how can you?" Jessie asked. "You can't see. I've got my derringer, don't forget. I'll get the drop on him—"

"No," Ki said. "It is too dangerous for you. One noise and he will awaken. You have only two shots, and there are four armed men to contend with. Even without my eyes, I am able to approach them more quietly than you could, and my blade is silent."

"You're right about that," Jessie admitted. "What do you want me to do?"

Ki, shrugging, turned his blind gaze in her direction.

"Have your little gun at the ready, in case I am not quiet enough."

Jessie gave him a quick hug. "There's crates and things scattered around. How will you get around them?" she asked worriedly.

"I will sense their presence," the samurai explained. "All the while, the rustlers' breathing will guide me."

"I could guide you—"

"No," Ki said firmly. "You would make too much noise. This is the only way. The task is mine to do."

"Please be careful," was all Jessie could say.

Ki flipped the *shuriken* into the air and caught it deftly. He tucked the blade into his back pocket, and smiled ruefully. "I do not see any problems."

Jessie watched him move off around the flour sacks, in the direction of the napping rustlers. She dug her derringer out of her boot and squeezed it nervously in her hands. Ki was advancing slowly and tentatively, obviously aware that one false move would be his last. His bare feet glided soundlessly across the dirt floor of the cavern. His arms were outstretched, his fingers spread and waving in the air. They reminded Jessie of a cat's whiskers.

Ki emptied his mind. Above his head, the kerosene lanterns burned on, but to the samurai they were of no more use than dim, twinkling stars on a fogbound, moonless night. Still, Ki was able to turn his blindness from a disadvantage to an advantage—he could not see, but that only meant he had one less distraction. He utilized every ounce of his awesome will to wipe away his concern for Jessie and the others, and even his own identity. He was no longer a samurai, or even a man. He was simply a force moving steadfastly through the universe, in perfect harmony with his surroundings. He was a rock rolling down a hill, a wave cascading upon the shore. These things need no eyes to find their way, for they are guided by the forces which permeate the world.

Ki's rational mind, his personality, glowed like an ember in the pit of his belly. His body moved of its own accord. His feet performed the *ko-ashi,* the "little step" that allowed the *te* adept to walk upon eggshell-thin china teacups without shattering them.

When Ki reached a crate in his path, he did not trip over the object, but paused just before it. The skin of his outstretched hands felt the change in air currents and temperature brought about by the obstacle's presence. Meticulously calibrated sidesteps, called *yoko-aruki,* took him no more than a fraction beyond the crate, and then he would resume his forward progress toward the guards, whose steady inhalations and exhalations reverberated in Ki's superbly focused sense of hearing. It was all a form of *zanshin,* or "feeling-moving" borrowed from the viper, which can slither toward its target by sensing the heat and vibrations emanating from its prey's body.

Ki was unaware of it, but his body was sheened with sweat from the enormous effort required of him to maintain the trance. No part of the consciousness that glowed in the pit of his stomach addressed itself to the question of how far he had come, or how far he still had to go. There was no coming or going. He had never left. He was already there.

"Papaaaa!"

Daniel's wail of terror tore Ki from his trance with sickening abruptness. It was as if the samurai had stumbled into a deep and icy pool of water.

"Papaaa!" the boy screamed again, jackknifing up into a sitting position. His eyes were wide and terror-struck as he snapped out of his nightmare.

Mary, bolting awake, hurried toward the boy. "What is

it? Child, what's wrong?" she cooed.

"B-bad dream," Daniel sobbed, burying his face against her chest.

Jessie stared at Danny and then back toward Ki. She herself was horror-stricken, but not by any dream. Ki was still some ten feet away from the closest of the rustlers, the dozing man who had been on sentry duty with his Winchester across his knees.

He was dozing no longer. His head had jerked up at Daniel's scream. "What the hell!" the rustler exclaimed as he stared unbelievingly at Ki. "Wake up, fellas!" he shouted, regaining his wits. "The chink's gotten loose!" As his partners stirred out of their drunken stupor, he himself brought up his Winchester.

Jessie tried to get a clear shot at him with her derringer, but Ki was standing in her line of fire. In any event, the rustler was a good thirty feet away. The distance was too great for her inaccurate little gun.

Ki focused on the metallic sound of the Winchester being cocked. He pulled his *shuriken* throwing blade from his pocket and hurled it in that direction. He allowed himself the satisfaction of listening to the *thunk!* of the blade as it embedded itself in the rustler's chest, the fatally wounded man's death rattle, and the clatter of his Winchester falling to the cavern's floor. Then the samurai crabbed sideways, throwing himself to the ground. His fingers touched a wooden crate, and he scurried behind it. Slugs slammed into the crate, jolting it against him as shots echoed off of the cavern's stone walls. The box wasn't very large, but Ki used *uzura gakure,* the escape technique in which one compressed one's body into a tight, round ball. In this way, Ki utilized every bit of cover the crate afforded. While he did so, the samurai wondered what his next move ought to be. He had no weapons, he could not see, and he was up against three armed men who were most likely even now converging upon him.

Jessie aimed, but did not fire at the trio of rustlers. They were still too far away for her derringer, especially since she had only two rounds. She stared in frustration at the Winchesters the men had left lying on the ground in their haste to attack Ki. They were blasting away at the crate he was hiding behind with their revolvers. If only she could get hold of one of those rifles.

She started to climb over the flour sacks, but one of the rustlers, seeing her, cried out, "Another one's loose!" He pegged a shot Jessie's way. It missed, sending up a white puff of dust as it punched into a flour sack, but it was enough to discourage her from trying to run across the open floor.

"Get down!" Mary scolded as she herself cowered beside Daniel. "It won't do Ki any good to get yourself killed!" The storekeeper's work-strengthened fingers had managed to pick apart the knots around Danny's wrists, and now the boy hurried to untie her hands.

Jessie hoisted herself up for another try at sprinting across the cavern in order to snatch up one of the rifles, but the rustlers' shots once again drove her down. This time she lost her footing, and toppled back behind the flour sacks. Her pratfall knocked the wind out of her, and for a moment she simply stared up at the rope-strung lanterns with stunned, blinking eyes.

The lanterns—they were all dangling from a single length of rope!

Jessie, still on her back, gripped with both hands and extended her arms straight up. As best she could, she sighted down the miniscule length of the stubby pistol, and fired the first of her two .38-caliber rounds. The derringer's report seemed no louder than a finger-snap amid the rifle fire. The stout manila rope stretching the length of the cavern was frayed where Jessie's bullet had nicked it, but still it held.

Calming herself, but nevertheless realizing that this chance would be her last, Jessie exhaled, steadied her aim, and gently squeezed the trigger. The derringer spat its last piece of lead. The rope pulled apart with a satisfying *twang!* The line of glowing lanterns crashed to the floor. The closest lantern landed on one of the flour sacks. The kerosene in its base ignited to spill tears of flame down the side of the burlap sack.

The three retreated from the burning liquid. "Ki!" Jessie shouted. "The lanterns are down!"

"Excellent!" Ki murmured to himself as he set off toward the three rustlers.

The cow thieves were stumbling and swearing, waving their pistols wildly in all directions. The lanterns' wicks had all winked out when the lanterns shattered. Here and there, small puddles of kerosene burned, but the light was fitful and wavering, and served only to destroy what little night vision the men might have developed. They blasted away at the tall shadows that now and again loomed against the stone walls. The noise of their guns, their own frightened shouts, and the screams of the horses in the rope corral only added to the confusion. A slowly running rivulet of burning kerosene reached a stack of wooden crates. Smoke began to fill the cavern as the dry wooden planking began to smolder and char.

"Stay down," Jessie warned her two companions. "We've got to wait until Ki gets rid of those men." She crouched down behind blackened, smoking flour sacks as bright blue muzzle flashes crisscrossed in the darkness.

"Can't—can't breathe," Danny gagged, coughing. "The smoke is burning my eyes!"

"We can't last here much longer," Mary added. "We'd better try to run for it."

"No!" Jessie said sharply. "Their aim might not be too good in all this confusion, but there's too much lead flying. And don't forget, Ki can't see. Right now he knows that anybody he comes across out there is fair game. That's the one advantage he has. If we start stumbling around, how will he know who to attack?"

"All right," Mary grumbled. "But he better get those thieves fast. I'd rather die by a bullet than choke to death on smoke!"

"Bud? Is that you?" one of the rustlers moaned. "I can't see a fucking thing!"

Grinning, Ki swerved nimbly to home in on the man's panic-stricken voice. He longed to get his hands on these three men who had manhandled and mistreated Jessie, Mary, and a defenseless young boy, and who had mocked his own blindness.

In the calm coastal waters of Ki's island homeland of Japan, there swim huge sharks that cruise just beneath the dark nighttime waves. During the summer, when the currents are balmy, people are tempted to indulge in moonlight swims. These individuals enjoy themselves, but they are wary. It often happens that a swimmer suddenly finds himself hauled down beneath the surface. He or she flails at the inky water, and wonders from which dim direction the shark will next attack.

These three rustlers are those hapless swimmers, Ki thought gleefully. *I am the shark.*

The man who had called out was lucky enough to see Ki materialize before him by the light of his pistol's muzzle blast. "Jesus!" the rustler screamed. He swung his heavy revolver in what he hoped was the direction of Ki's head. The rustler knew that the "Chinaman" was too close to shoot. His only hope was that he could club the bastard to death—

Ki heard the whistle of the handgun through the air as it arced toward his scalp. He protected his upper body by bringing up his left arm in a rising block. The pistol's barrel slashed down upon his forearm, but the samurai's sinewy muscles were like plates of steel thinly cushioned with cotton padding. He never felt the rustler's desperate blow. Instead, Ki countered with the most deadly attack in his entire *te* arsenal: the *choku-zuki*, an intensely focused, short, straight thrust.

Ki's clenched right fist shot straight out at chest height. The thrust had begun with Ki's palm turned up, but as the punch traveled toward his adversary, the samurai corkscrewed his fist around so that it landed in a palm-down position at the focus of the blow. The corkscrew movement was originally perfected by the ancient blind monks of

Okinawa. The movement's effectiveness was twofold. First, it created shockwaves that added to the penetrating strength of the punch. Second, backed by the *kime*, or focused energy of the *te* adept, the corkscrewing movement created a momentary vacuum, so that the target was literally sucked toward the onrushing fist.

Ki's knuckles slammed into the rustler's sternum. There was a wet *crunch!* and then just the slightest whistle as the man exhaled his last, dying breath. The rustler did not have time to scream before he slumped to the floor, his heart as savaged by Ki's blow as it would have been by a bullet.

A second rustler stumbled into Ki. The samurai drove his elbow into the man's belly, and then took two steps forward to execute a backward foot-thrust, the heel of his striking foot catching the rustler's knee. The man's leg snapped like a brittle twig, and he dropped, screaming, to the floor.

There was one last man at large in the cavern, but Ki could not waste any more time looking for him. The samurai's keen hearing had told him that Jessie, Mary, and Danny had not tried to escape. They could afford to wait no longer. The smoke was chokingly thick.

"Jessie!" he called out. "Run for it, now!" Even as he spoke, a stack of smoldering crates burst into flame. The fire crackled merrily, and was so bright that Ki had to shield his still blind, but increasingly sensitive eyes.

"Come on!" Jessie yelled. She and Mary flanked the coughing, crying Danny. Each woman held one of the boy's hands. They stumbled blindly. The fire gave them enough light to see by, but the acrid black fog of smoke stung their eyes, blurring their vision with streaming tears. The trio were halfway across the cavern's floor when the smoke momentarily cleared. Jessie spotted the last rustler just in front of the horses' rope corral. She looked around wildly, searching for a weapon as the man spotted them and brought up his pistol. At her feet was one of the Winchesters.

"Run for it!" she ordered Mary and Danny. The two hesitated. The rustler fired. His bullet whizzed past Jessie's ear. "Go on!" she cried. "Take off!" She snatched up the rifle and stayed in a half-crouch, levering off two rounds from the hip. The .44-40 slugs knocked the rustler backward. He fell across the rope holding the milling horses against the cavern's far wall. The man's dead weight pulled the rope barricade down. The fear-crazed horses stampeded. They'd been in and out of the cavern countless times, and knew which way to go.

"Watch out!" Jessie cried. Mary and Danny threw themselves to one side as the four horses barreled down the corridor that led to the mine's front entrance.

Jessie felt a hand on her shoulder. She spun around, already levering a new round into the Winchester's chamber, even as she heard Ki say, "Don't shoot!"

She hugged the samurai. "How did you find me?"

"You've been screaming bloody murder!" His chuckle turned into a painful, racking cough. "You'd better lead us out."

"But which way?" Jessie asked as impenetrable billows of smoke swirled around them.

"I was hoping you could tell me that," Ki said wryly. "You're the one who can see."

"The place is filled with smoke!" Jessie cried. Just then there came the sound of wood splintering. One end of the cavern lit up, the smoke turning from black to luminous, pearly gray.

"The horses," Jessie laughed. "They've kicked the outer door down!"

"As I remember, those double doors were fairly rickety," Ki nodded. "Not like horses to kick through wood panels, but when they are faced with the choice of smashing down doors or burning to death—"

"They kick!" Jessie agreed. "Come on! It must be high noon outside. There's enough sunlight to show us the way!"

Jessie led Ki across the floor and down the tunnel. Once outside, she saw Mary and Danny sprawled on the sparse, yellow-green, prickly grass. They were grinning and breathing deeply in the fresh, sunlit air.

"We're all safe," Jessie laughed with relief. She dropped her Winchester and collapsed next to Daniel, tousling his hair and hugging him.

"Help! Help me!" echoed a cry from inside the mine. "Somebody! I don't wanna burn!"

"It is that man who I disabled, but did not kill," Ki sighed. "His leg is broken." The samurai started back toward the entrance of the smoke-filled cavern.

"Wait!" Mary cried. "Jessie! Stop him! He can't go back in there! They've stockpiled tins of kerosene. If that stuff catches . . ." She shook her head. "He doesn't have to risk his life—"

"Yes he does," Daniel said, so quietly that both women had to strain to hear him. "He can't let a man who's calling for help die. It wouldn't be honorable."

They all watched the samurai stumble his way toward the smoky entrance. "Shouldn't one of us go with him?" Mary demanded.

"No," Jessie said dully, watching her friend disappear into the dark opening. "He wouldn't allow it. He'd just say, 'Why should two of us risk our lives?'"

They waited and watched for an anxious minute that seemed to last an hour. Finally they spotted Ki in the mine's entranceway. The samurai was slumped against the stone wall. The rustler was in his arms, and was holding on to Ki for dear life. He was hugging Ki so tightly, both in fear and gratitude, that he resembled a bride being carried across the threshold.

"Hurry!" Jessie called frantically. "The kerosene!"

But Ki could not hurry. Even a samurai's strength has its limits. Smoke filled Ki's lungs, and his muscles ached from exertion. He stumbled against a stone in his path as the full-grown, heavyset, writhing man in his arms clutched at him in savage hysteria.

"Just a few more feet!" Jessie shouted, and began to run to him.

The explosion of the kerosene tins sounded like a deep,

guttural grunt as it reverberated inside the thick stone walls of the mine. A tongue of flame licked out from the entrance, singeing the back of Ki's clothing. The hot blast of air lifted the samurai up, tumbling him through space. He'd absorbed most of the shock of the explosion, his own body protecting the rustler who had been in his arms. Ki could hear the man shrieking, but then he himself slammed down against the ground, the force of the landing knocking him unconscious.

Jessie had thrown up her hands to protect her face during the explosion. The force of the blast seemed to shake the earth. Jessie toppled sideways, the breath knocked out of her, but she was crawling toward Ki's limp body on her hands and knees as thick plumes of pitch-black smoke boiled out from the mine opening.

"He saved me!" the rustler was blubbering, even as he winced in pain from his broken leg. "That crazy chink saved my goddamned life!"

Mary and Daniel peered down as Jessie cradled Ki's head in her lap. "How is he?" the storekeeper asked anxiously.

"Out cold," Jessie murmured. She looked up at Mary. "We've got to get him to a doctor."

Danny, pointing toward the west, said, "We've got company. Riders, a whole bunch of 'em. Coming fast."

"Can you make them out?" Jessie asked worriedly, and when the boy shook his head, she instructed, "Fetch that Winchester. Mary, see if the thief that Ki saved has a gun."

The woman did as she was told. "His holster's empty, but he's one of the pair who got the jump on us back in the cave. He's still got *your* Colt tucked in his waistband." She relieved the injured man of Jessie's weapon, and hurried back with it in order to make a stand, along with Danny, around Jessie and the fallen samurai.

"Holy cow!" the boy sputtered. "We are in for it! I see old man Schiff himself in the lead. And next to him is the one named Tim!" He checked to make sure that there was a round in the Winchester's chamber. "Tim's the one who bragged about shooting my father . . ."

"Hold your fire, both of you!" Jessie commanded. "I see Deputy Stills riding with them! And there's Deputy Oakley!"

In all, the posse was made up of twenty men, and most of them were citizens of Nettle Grove, as Jessie could tell by their clothing and weaponry. It seemed as if the two deputies had hastily raided every store and office in the township, swearing in aproned shopkeepers and black-suited lawyers and arming them with scatterguns and old Colt Dragoons left over from the Civil War. The towns-folk looked supremely uncomfortable after their long, hard ride.

"What's happened?" Stills drawled as he dismounted. His mustard-colored cow pony dipped its scrawny neck and began to graze the tough-bladed prickly grass. "How bad is your friend hurt?" the deputy asked.

"I can't tell," Jessie fretted. She managed a faint smile for the lawman. "I see you've got your badge back."

"Yep. The doc was wrong about Marshal Forbes being out for a day." Stills's brown eyes crinkled with amusement. "What he forgot was that the marshal drinks a pint of bourbon every night, and still manages to wake up for duty at six in the morning. That medicine only kept him out for an hour, and when he came to, he straightaway cleared me of shooting him."

"That's right, Miss Starbuck," Oakley volunteered from his saddle. "I done apologized to Hank, and he became head deputy all over again."

"We found the gunslick who *did* shoot Forbes lying dead in the stable," Stills continued. "Your rented horse was gone, Jessie, so I figured you'd lit out for Skinny Creek, like we'd planned." He gestured back toward the ragtag posse. "I swore in all the men I could find on short notice, and we set out on your trail. Met up with Mr. Schiff and a few of his boys on the way." Stills winked at Jessie. "I haven't had a chance to talk to him yet," he added.

The gray-haired cattle baron took off his silver-conchoed hat and wiped at his brow. He looked glum about meeting up with the posse. He was still dressed in his green corduroy suit, but this time he had a Colt strapped about his waist. He and the four mounted men surrounding him kept their horses a little bit apart from the main body of the posse. "It looks like everything is under control here, Deputy," Schiff mumbled. "So we'll be on our way."

"Not so fast," Mary said. "Deputy? This here young fellow is Daniel Tang." She rested her hand on the boy's shoulder.

"He and all the rest of us have been held prisoner by the rustlers who've been using this mine as a hideout." She pointed to the riders grouped around Schiff. "*Those* fellas are the rest of the gang!"

"Ignore her!" Schiff sputtered angrily. "Stills, you work in my town! You'll do as I say—" The cattleman's face flushed red, and his watery blue eyes glared in fury. "Tim here has been with me for years—"

"He's the one who shot my pa!" Danny cried out, tearing loose from Mary's restraining hand. He ran forward, dragging the stock of the Winchester behind him through the grass, to point an accusing finger. "He's Tim! He's the one that did it!"

"Shut up, you little brat!" Tim snarled. He made to reach for his gun, but Schiff grabbed his hand, muttering, "Don't be a fool."

"That's good advice, Tim," Stills drawled. "I'm placing you under arrest."

As Tim stared dumbly, Schiff smiled down at the tall, blond deputy. "Hank, be reasonable," the cattleman began. "It's that boy's word against mine, and I'll swear that Tim had nothing to do with any murders or rustling or whatever." He looked around at his other men and beamed magnanimously. "I'll vouch for all four of my boys here. Now who's going to call Tom Schiff a liar in his own town?"

"I will!"

All eyes turned toward the rustler Ki had rescued.

"Bud!" Tim wailed. "You'll get us all hanged!"

"Don't care," the injured rustler said stubbornly. "These folks saved me from burnin' up. When I was trapped in that mine I prayed to God. I promised that iffen I was saved, I'd repent my evil ways. Well, I was saved, and now I'm repentin'!"

"Good for you, Bud," Mary cheered.

"Deputy," the rustler went on, "I'll testify that old man Schiff ordered us to rustle cows. He even said to kill Hiram Tang, iffen we could."

"Oh, Jesus," Tim groaned softly. "Bud, you killed us."

"We tied up all these good folks as well," the hurt rustler continued. "And I'll swear to the whole damned thing in court!"

"Well now, Mr. Schiff," Stills said, his hands on his hips. "I'd say things are starting to come together. I've got witnesses, and I've got the motive—"

"What? What's that?" Schiff stammered. He looked like he'd aged ten years in the last few minutes. "W-what motive could I possibly have?" The cattle baron tried to laugh, but it came out more like a sick wheeze.

"Tom," Stills began softly, "we got the paper out of your vault. The paper that proves you accepted fifty thousand in cash from foreigners in exchange for Hiram Tang's mineral rights."

"I. . . I . . ." Schiff's voice trailed off.

"Tom Schiff, " Stills called out in a firm, clear voice. "I'm arresting you and your four men. Now all of you drop your gunbelts!"

"Tim!" Schiff cried out in an old man's wavering voice. "Get me out of this!" The cattle baron wheeled his horse around hard, and lit out, kneeing his mount into a full run.

Tim drew his pistol and send a shot in Stills's direction. The round kicked up a spurt of dust between the deputy's boots as Stills drew his own .44 and fired twice. His slugs caught Tim in the chest, knocking the man from his saddle to lie sprawled in the dirt. The rustler kicked once, and then lay still. The three other cow thieves took one look at the fifteen guns the posse was pointing their way, and quickly raised their hands in surrender.

"Oakley," Stills sighed, "get on after Mr. Schiff and—"

The deputy was cut off by the sound of a rifle shot. He turned to watch Schiff clutch at his spine and cartwheel off his loping horse. The cattle baron hit the ground hard, sending up a cloud of dust.

Danny dropped the smoking Winchester. "He's the one who really killed my pa," he said softly, his eyes wet with tears. "He's the one made me an orphan . . ." He began to sob.

Mary ran to the boy and hugged him tight. "Just hush," she murmured against the boy's crying. "You ain't no orphan. Why, you got me to look out for you! I'll be your ma *and* your pa, you'll see. Hush now, just hush . . ."

Stills, nodding wearily, only repeated, "Oakley, get on after Mr. Schiff."

"Ain't no need to hurry," the bearded deputy grumbled. "Mr. Schiff ain't going nowhere." He nudged his horse into a walk toward the cattle baron's body.

Jessie, meanwhile, had been kneeling next to Ki, watching for signs of consciousness. As the samurai began to moan softly, she called out excitedly, "He's coming out of it!"

Mary, holding Danny against her side, walked with the boy over to where Jessie was kneeling.

"Just take it easy," Jessie soothed the samurai, gently stroking his forehead. "Rest, we'll get you a doctor . . ."

Ki opened his eyes, and cried out in pain. His first conscious thought was that he was still in the mine and had caught fire, for how else could he explain the burning brightness stabbing into his eyes? He brought his hand up to shield his face. Jessie caught hold of his fingers and gently pulled them away. Ki stared into her face, into her wet green eyes, and smiled.

"Jessie, do not cry," he whispered. "I can see . . ." A boy knelt down beside him and clutched at his other hand. Ki looked into the face of a reed-thin, red-haired young fellow whose nose and cheeks were sprinkled with freckles.

"Danny," Ki smiled.

"Yes, sir?" the boy replied, squeezing Ki's hand for dear life.

"You look just like your father, boy," Ki chuckled.

Danny broke into a wide grin. "That's what everyone says."

Ki nodded as best he could with his head still cradled in Jessie's lap. He closed his aching eyes against the bright noonday sun. "Good to see you, Danny," the samurai murmured, and then he went back to sleep.

★

Chapter 14

Marshal Forbes's desk had been jammed up against the wall which displayed his office's ragged collection of wanted posters. In the desk's place was a folding cot borrowed from one of the jail cells. The marshal himself, his side plastered over with white tape, lounged on the cot like a king on his throne. A quart bottle of bonded bourbon rested beside him. He kept filling his glass and drinking steadily as he listened to Stills's recounting of the previous day's events at Skinny Creek. When the deputy was done, Forbes lifted his glass in a toast.

"To you, Miss Starbuck, the prettiest little lady in Wyoming. And to you, Hank. Why, you wrapped this case up as good as I ever could."

"Why, thank you, Cal," Stills replied. He and Jessie exchanged amused glances as they sipped at their drinks.

"And I'm glad things worked out for you, Ki," the marshal nodded. "Sure you won't have a little drink?"

"Thank you, but no," Ki replied. "I'm still not totally recovered from my experience." He fingered his many-pocketed leather vest. "Although I must say that regaining my blades, bow, and arrows has done much to restore my spirits."

"Weren't nothing to it," Forbes grinned. "Found that stuff out at Schiff's ranch. Reckon his rustlers brought it to him as proof they'd done you in." The marshal squinted at Ki, and then held up two fingers. "How many, son?"

"Quite amusing," the samurai said, smiling thinly.

"Strangest damn thing I ever heard of," Forbes marveled. "If the doc himself hadn't told me, I wouldn't have believed it. A bullet takes your sight away, and an explosion brings it back. Let's drink to a miracle!" He raised his glass.

"Hardly a miracle," Ki replied evenly. "My vision was temporarily impaired by a concussion. The explosion's shockwave sufficiently jarred the optic nerve to relieve the pressure upon it. It was subsiding on its own, in any event."

"Optic what?" Forbes shook his head. "He's always talk like that?" he asked Jessie.

"Always," she shrugged.

"Like *how?*" Ki asked, and then decided that the bourbon had gone to their heads as they burst into laughter.

"Marshal," Jessie asked, "I take it there won't be any problem about Daniel's having shot Tom Schiff?"

"Well now," Forbes grumbled. "The kid's technically guilty of manslaughter or some damned thing," he shrugged. "But that's according to the law books, and here in Nettle Grove we put the Good Book before any other volume. The Old Testament says an eye for an eye. Tom Schiff done in Danny's father, more or less. Danny done old Tom in." He winked at Jessie. "Guess I got enough on my plate without going around poking up trouble where there ain't none."

"Well, that brings us back to the business that originally brought me here," Jessie smiled. "Mary Hudson is going to be moving in with Daniel at his ranch. We got the judge to appoint her as the boy's guardian."

"Excellent!" Ki repeated. "She and Danny need each other. She will help him get over the loss of his father, and he can fill the place left by the loss of her family."

"Mary's a good worker," Stills added. "Between them they ought to be able to run their spread."

"I agree," Jessie said. "That's why I signed the agreements Hiram and I had drawn up. The Starbuck organization can now proceed with the financial backing we promised the small ranchers."

"Yep," Forbes said shrewdly. "Only thing Danny needs now is a father." The marshal stared at Stills, who quickly began to blush. "Somebody's promised to ride by now and then to give that gal a hand, I've heard tell."

"Why, Hank Stills!" Jessie pretended to scold. "You never told me you liked blue-eyed women!"

"If I can't have green..." the deputy drawled. Then it was Jessie's turn to blush.

"Only one last problem," Forbes mused. "We got fifty thousand dollars and a whole lotta cattle, both of which used to belong to Schiff. The old skinflint was too cold to ever take a wife. He's got no heirs. What about those assets?"

"It's been taken care of," Jessie blurted, glad to get the subject off women's eyes, and back to business.

"How so?" Stills asked.

Jessie glanced at Ki, who smiled back. "Well," she began, "the judge has agreed that the money Schiff got from the Prussians should be used to buy breeding stock for all the ranchers in the vicinity, both big and small. It's time the cattlemen in this part of Wyoming started working together. How else are you folks ever going to get to be a state?"

"Yes, ma'am," Forbes chuckled, bowing his head in Jessie's direction. "That's a fine idea, Miss Starbuck."

"What about the cattle?" Stills asked.

"They go to Danny," Jessie said firmly. "Cows are a poor exchange for the loss of his father, but it's the best we can do."

Forbes sighed and nodded. "Prussians was behind all this

trouble, you say?" His face grew dark. "I ain't but a town marshal, ma'am, but I'd love to get them Prussian fellas in *my* jail!"

Jessie smiled. "They've been punished fifty thousand dollars' worth, I reckon."

"But do they know it?" Forbes asked.

"They will!" Jessie laughed richly, her green eyes sparkling with mischief. "I intend to send a letter overseas to the business address listed on that contract Schiff had hidden in his vault." She paused. "Now that I'm thinking about it, I'll send along the contract as well, just to prove to them that I'm not bluffing, that we really did foil their fifty-thousand-dollar scheme!"

"But Jessie," Ki laughed, "the Prussians will know that anyway, when they glimpse your business stationery."

"I don't get it," Forbes muttered.

"The stationery is embossed with the Circle Star insignia," Ki explained. "The Prussians have learned to fear the worst when they are confronted with the Starbuck brand!"

Watch for

LONE STAR IN THE TALL TIMBER

seventh in the hot new
LONE STAR series from Jove
coming in January!